PRAISE FOR OTHER WOI

C000052868

'What a fabulous book, hard boiled crime
intoxicatingly hard to swallow and a story that has sharp edges, it's like
swallowing a jagged bottle that's been used to glass you whilst reading.'
— **Ross Jeffery**, author of *Juniper*

'Bowie's offerings are hard to swallow, but swallow you must, because this is
the rise of what I believe will be a powerhouse in crime writing for years to come.
'It is a cocktail of delight and one that needs to be sipped and savoured, and
after reading it, it leaves you punch drunk and stumbling around on your feet
– hard hitting and oh so good.
'The dirty realism of Bukowski, Fante, and McCarthy; then you have the best
of noir writing from Raymond Chandler, James Ellroy and Paul D. Brazill,
plus the flair of J.G. Ballard.
'A masterful series that has all the power of reincarnated greats of the genre –
a devastating book full of dirty realism that pulls you into the undertow, try
as you might to rise, it will pull you under and into a world that you can't
escape from, an immersive must read!'
— **Storgy Magazine**

'This book is the three D's, dark - deep and dirty!
'It's not for the faint hearted yet somehow manages to balance lyrical and
poetic beauty with hard realism and violence which sometimes can make you
uncomfortable. The book takes you on an underworld journey with the
protagonist - every step of the sometimes ethereal way. I haven't read another
book like it and look forward to the next instalment!'
— **Alison B**

'Dirty Realism, Beautifully Written - Lived every page, loved every page!'
— **Jax**

'This book is amazing. A modern noir classic with gritty characters and a very realistic plot. The author puts you right in the front seat of a bus speeding through the 90s Bristol club and pub scene. It's really vivid, you will experience every pint and punch as if you were really there on the dance floor when it's way past 'respectable 0 clock'. The book is a complete story in itself but I can't wait for the follow up. The main character is destined to be a literary hero somewhere between Philip Marlowe and Patrick Bateman. 'I bought this book because it's set in Bristol, reading about real pubs and clubs that you might know adds a new dimension to the reading experience. Why don't more authors write like this?'

— **Robert Salad**

'This is a tough read, with the storyline revolving around a very bored John, trapped in a life which is his unwelcome reward for having been a good citizen, suddenly reinventing himself with the assistance of liberal (some might say, excessive) amounts of alcohol. A mystery is thrust upon him by a neighbour. Will he succeed in solving it? Well, you might need a drink or two to find out!'

— **Tom Henry**

'John, the protagonist of Untethered, is a man with a dark and secret past who is living a new life under witness protection. As he sits alone in his flat, drinking and writing in his journal, John becomes embroiled in the search for a missing neighbour.

'John Bowie's '90s set Untethered is a violent and intense read. Lyrical, moody, funny and as gritty as hell, Untethered is like a British blend of Jim Thompson and Nelson Algren.'

— **Paul D. Brazill**, author of *Small Time Crimes*

'I always know a great piece of writing by a great author because as a writer myself while I'm reading the damn thing I'm jealous as hell. *Transference* by John Bowie made me jealous A LOT. So many great lines followed by greater lines. *Transference* is a bleak, beautiful ode to Manchester.'

— **Stephen J. Golds**, author of *Always The Dead*

'Enter the heart of darkness. Truly spellbinding.
'I don't often read books in one extended sitting - but this was just too good to put down!
'If you like taut, lyrical, gritty noir, then *Transference* is for you. Bowie takes you on a trip back to the days when 90s Manchester aka Madchester to tourists like me, was rarely out of the headlines. Enter the heart of darkness, the local's bars and seedy clubs, then bounce off the walls, out into darker alleys, and along sinister canal towpaths littered with junkies, pushers and wanna-be chav gangsters. The protagonist John Black, is a man seeking redemption for his past life, seeking to write the wrongs that haunt his dreams. A writer/private investigator, Black is compelled to face off with his former gangland boss, now in pole position as Manchester's Mr Big.
'It's the second book in the *Black Viking* Thriller series but could also be read as a stand-alone book, such is the brilliance of the writing - and with our protagonist and Bowie's expert and masterful storytelling we have a series and a protagonist that we can enjoy for many outings to come!'

— **MJ Newman**, author of the *Crime Syndicate Series*

JOHN BOWIE

John's writing has appeared online and in print for the likes of *Red Dog Press, Bristol Noir, Storgy Magazine, Close to the Bone, Litro Magazine, Punk Noir Magazine, Necro Productions* and *Deadman's Tome.*

He writes poetry, short stories, and novels. His fiction is a semi-autobiographical mix of dirty realism, crime fiction and noir. Ghostly references to a heritage that includes the Vikings, Scotland, Ireland and the North, U.K. flavour the words throughout. Often with a dark humoured edge.

He's the founder and editor of the Bristol Noir e-zine which specialises in dirty realism, noir, and dark fiction. Past contributors include some of the best established and emerging writers in these fields.

John lives in Bristol with his wife and daughters, where he has been since the late nineties. He is a professional designer, artist, and writer as well as a proud husband, father, brother, and son.

John's first novel, *Untethered,* the first in the Black Viking Thriller series is out now with Red Dog Press. Three follow ups are due throughout 2021.

His poetry collection, *Dead Birds & Sinking Ships (Little Tales of Melancholy Madness)* is slated for June 2021 with Close to the Bone Publishing.

And a collection of Bristol Noir stories (*Tainted Hearts & Dirty Hellhounds*) curated by and including John's work, is slated for 2021.

WESTON – SUPER NIGHTMARE

A Hellbent Riff Raff Thriller

by
John Bowie

Close To The Bone
An imprint of Gritfiction Ltd

Copyright © 2021 by John Bowie

First published in Great Britain in 2021 by Close To The Bone

ISBN 979-8-5930-7036-4

All rights reserved. No part of the book may be produced in any form
or by any electronic or mechanical means, including information
storage and retrieval systems, without permission in writing from the
publisher, except by a reviewer who may use brief quotations in a book
review.

Close To The Bone
an imprint of Gritfiction Ltd
Rugby
Warwickshire
United Kingdom
CV21
www.close2thebone.co.uk

The characters and events in this book are fictitious. Any similarity to
real persons, living or dead, is coincidental and not intended by the
author.

Interior Design by Craig Douglas
Cover by John Bowie

First Printing, 2021

For
Mademoiselle Pamplemousse

"I've got the blues in my heart, and the Devil in my fingers."
— Angus Young, **ACDC**

WESTON—SUPER
NIGHTMARE

One

JIMI PLAYED GUITAR. He was okay, not great. They had to listen… His fearsome bald head banged away as the feedback and Gibson SG rasps tore the place *a new one* every night. The Hell's Belles was his bar, and if they didn't like it, they knew what could do, and fuck right off.

Once, some American tourists talked over one of his solos. Why they were in Weston-super-Mare, who knows. He'd have liked to meet the guy that sold them that holiday: Quaint British Victorian seaside resort. Lovely promenade, with entertainment on the Grand Pier. Locally caught and cooked cuisine. Donkey rides on the beach…

All bollocks.

In reality, it was mudflats, junkies, whores, drunks, and angry seagulls wrestling you for soggy chips from a squeaky polystyrene tray. All this with a backdrop of rundown penny arcades, greasy spoons, and charity shops. As they say: charity begins at home. And back then, the town needed it like a junky needs a fix.

There they were, these naive Yanks; talking shit, leant up against *his* bar.

Brazen as fuck.

And there *he* was, giving it some: 'Whole Lotta Rosie'.

Next morning the police found them under the pier buried up to their necks. Five children's coloured buckets placed over their heads. They couldn't remember a thing except for some god-awful guitar solo…so they said. The Police knew fine well who was behind it and left *him* well alone. They liked their end of shift drinks in Jimi's bar more than they liked the tourists that seemed to descend on the place every year in droves. Like the ravenous seagulls, pecking and scrounging at every scrap the tourists swept through and shat on it. And it was the police left to clear up after.

Jimi had a few names in that town. Tour Guide wasn't one of them and when the sun went down, one sort headed straight to his place; a handful of regulars would be there propping up the bar already. The others...got as far away as possible. For their lives and reputations sake. It was the Wild West alright. And, although he had somehow got a crazy reputation for putting a name on a few, this wasn't Tombstone.

'Why d' you have to go do that?' Tammy asked as her sandy blonde hair, bleached into streaks by the sun, moved a little on each word. As if the wind was on her side, helping to break through to Jimi.

'Didn't like those Yanks. Spoilt my best bit. Roughed up and roofied them a little — wee teaser — no harm.'

'No, I meant why you go letting them live?'

They laughed through the night, 'till morning. When she had a mouthful of him under the pier at sunset, she was still giggling about it. Tickled him along all the more.

'Careful there. Might blow my sack up. Float me out to sea.'

She winked, finished him off. And they sat, watching the sun cast blood orange flames over those tainted murky waves.

Drips of a day's already forgotten detritus fell from the piers underbelly, making way for the new day. 'This town'll never change,' she said to the sea as a seagull wrestled a rubber johnny by a once ornate pillar.

'Hope not... an' if it does, we won't. The bar neither,' Jimi said to the sand, dropping his Marlboro Red and scrubbing it into a child's sandy discarded sock with his foot.

They paused in respite as a fragment of calm washed over them with a whiff of last night's vinegar on chips, stale beer on clothes, and the morning's first fresh dog shit on the sand.

'Matt wants to play…' she said after a while. She'd waited, had picked her moment to drop the bomb. His gun was empty, his testosterone recharging as a cocktail of post-climax brain chemicals was calming a beast.

He took it in, waiting himself, knowing his reaction would turn a tide.

'Ee's too good… Tell 'im to try Big T's place instead. They go in for all that Craps-got Talent, X Fuck-tor shite in there,' and with that, he put a stake in the ground. Fate changed direction; down another dirty alley.

'Already have, pet,' she said, 'Just thought I'd check. As you know who his brothers are.'

'Passed harder turds… I'm done with all that.'

'You could have moved further away. Bristol… Cardiff...are only there,' and she waved at two imagined points in the distance. A distance meant to hide a reputation and connections.

He'd done nothing really bad since arriving in town… Since he'd driven his Transit van down there full of a hard life's possessions close to a decade ago. With only the two-seater sofa (no cushions), old black 'n white TV, fishing rods, a claw and ball-pein hammer for company.

In the cities, he was The Man, The Mark, and Mr Cig — a hard grafter. The best builder and general labourer there was. The gangland bosses and runners would drink with him at the local boozer: The Cornubia. Noisy damn parrot in there didn't give him any respect but the rest did. He was known as the man for getting stuff done. He was a fucking ox.

Now, in Weston, he'd become J. T. Trouser snake or Jimi Strings. On account of his playing and the massive bulge; carried on and off stage. He still did favours for mates: *this* and *that*. Fixing *this* on a house or a caravan, repairing *that* on a shop or arcade. Or, knocking a cocky lad out that was bothering someone's daughter.

He kept a barrier of comfort close to him made up of Tammy and Betty. Both big city dropouts too, street smart strumpets from the bigger smoke. Drawn by a slower pace. Easier lives with the background sounds of waves in the background to soothe a life full of mistakes and bad judgements. Tammy's tattoos covered *some* of the track marks on her arms and Betty's arse still twinged every time she went up and down the steps to the beer cellar. Those age-old stitches had long since dissolved — the memories remained, stinging like vinegar to a paper cut with each step. They'd both done hard time. Come out the other side. Jimi looked after them. A real man. Full of floored sensitivities. But none of these hang-ups was taken out on the girls. And they looked after each other and him. Real strong women. Albeit if Betty, technically used to be a man. Something she'd whisper in the sweaty city suit's ears, in the lap dancing joint, just as they were about to pop. She'd dance and grind, working them up so they were all hot and bothered. That confused look on their faces that came each time, when she dropped the bomb, was forever imprinted on to her memory. She could see them all fresh as the day it happened. And she kept them, recalling them when she needed a little pick me up and a giggle. It was a reminder of how grim it used to be. And how sweet it was now.

The painted steel sign above the door of their bar, The Hell's Belles, said:

'Come in for a stiff one. It's ladies night.
EVERY NIGHT!'

***

Betty Jardin was the official Hell's Belles barmaid with orbs like canons and raven black straight hair. They left the punter flirting to her, whilst Jimi and Tammy tended the doors and entertainment; personally. Other than a token flash of Betty's guns during Jimi's set. Who didn't like that? The shirttail lifters were welcome. Of course, they added to the open to all multicoloured anarchy of the place. Without them, it wouldn't work either. Betty's secret, 'tucked away' past was an in-joke with them too, they knew about it and laughed at the leering idiots who only saw what they wanted to see. And that's how Betty wanted it. Proud of the power hidden in her transformation into true self. Jimi had been in a few gay bars; didn't complain about what he saw. Kind of liked it. He didn't expect any moaning the other way around.

It was his place. His rules.

As far as he was concerned he'd had it made. No more calluses on his palms for pennies. Now, just on his fingertips now from the strings. He drank what he wanted, fiddled the figures. The brewery had long since stopped supplying the disappearing Jack D. Leaving him, Betty, and Tammy to top up the bottles from the wholesalers when they ran low.

Spit and sawdust?

This place was concrete, blood and sweat.

It was beautiful.

A multi-coloured, tit-filled barrel of his own making and he dived right in every night.

Two

'I REALLY WANNA PLAY,' Matt said, smiling, the next morning.

'Nope. Not good enough. He told me last night,' said Tammy. Not even bothering to look round from the cash register. She could see his seedy, crooning smirk in the mirror and she didn't want it in her face.

'Really,' he slurred.

She took a nip from a shot glass that was always there in case they needed it. None of them had much of a traditional customer service background and sometimes they needed *a little help*.

'Why you wanna play anyway. You know the way it works in here? Just him and the girls. Always has been…' she said over a shoulder.

'*Has beens* is fucking right,' he cut in. 'Thought I'd inject a bit of class into the place, didn't I.'

'Keep talking like that and I'll go get him over. He had some bad news about his mother last night. Been drinking Jacky D straight-up since he found out… Won't be the best company,' she said, pointing to the hunched shadow sat on the edge of the stage.

A dull glimmer of light bounced from the bald sullen skull topping his silhouetted mass.

Matt could see Jimi. A shape. The mass of hurt.

Jimi had an empty steel stare as if at any moment his clenched fist would destroy the tumbler he held, and it would shatter, smashing, and spill an eternity of dead relatives on to the floor in front of him with his own blood.

He dropped it. Smash. And he was lost in a dark illusion laid out before him by an impending loss.

Matt jumped at the breaking glass.

'Forget it. We'll be back. After he's on his feet,' he said gesturing at the shadows. She knew what he meant by *we*. It'd be him and his weird-assed brothers next — the fucked-up quartet.

'He's never left his feet. What you see there is a hard bastard — havin' breakfast. Now, fuck off,' she said and pointed to the door.

She locked up behind him.

Tammy knew better...hadn't actually seen him emotionally touched this much in their time together. She did know his estranged son was a no-go area. That and a tattoo of a ladies name he carried, seemed to regret, but other than slicing across it himself with a bottle one night, didn't do much to him. He wouldn't have it properly removed. No, nothing much seemed to touch him...not like this. Other than her, and sometimes Betty, when Tammy let her get involved — and he fancied it.

'Another?' she said. They'd given Betty the day off whilst he came to terms with the soon to be cropped family tree.

So, she served.

And he drank through it.

The lights dimmed outside and inside they came slowly up to a dull orange.

***

By 7 pm he was at the back, pretending to do the setlist. The paper and pen in front of him were a blur. He only saw loss. It'd be the same as always anyway. Nothing to figure out. The sets always consisted of two-thirds him, one-third Tammy. And Betty would dance on the bar, get them out — flashing those double bangers.

No set change. Not tonight. Everyone would be happy, but for once not him.

The gangsters' kid brother could pain some other ears — not ours, he thought.

They opened the door.

'We're opening you up… Jimi,' the first of the three brothers said through the crack of the door.

They hovered in the doorway.

'And now, we're coming in,' he continued. He had a nickname: *The Narrator*. All of them did… Oddballs, all three were known as: *The Narrator, The Echo* and *Last Orders*.

'Coming in…and taking a seat,' The second one, The Echo said.

'We're taking a seat and you're gonna listen,' Last Orders, finished.

Jimmy looked up.

He Sobered.

Hard and unflinching at their presence, the pains and drunkenness dripped out of each pore. Each step towards where he sat brought them, *all* of them, nearer to war.

'You boys must be due for retirement, the way you're headed. Bored of coming down heavy on the slots, sluts, and easy landlords? If you want out, just say the word.'

'Jimmy, Jimmy, Jimmy… Play nice. We've always left you alone. Stayed to our side and left you to yours. Our boy Matty-boy just wants to play,' The Narrator said, pointing to a silhouette outside, like a schoolboy outside class as parents checked up on a misbehaving teacher.

'Wants to play…'

'… Play.'

'There's a *dull echo* in here, don't you think?' Jimi said.

'Now then… Easy. We won't expect payment. The kid just wants a go on *your* stage. Just ease off on the hard rock shit for a night and let some real talent have a go,' Last

Orders gestured to Matt who was now leant smirking in the doorway. A toothpick hanging from his perfect TV smile.

Jimmy knew better.

This was power play.

Let another man on your stage, stealing your thunder and next thing you know, he'd be riding the girls and making you watch.

No, not here. Not in this bar.

This was Jimi's place.

The three brothers, plus Matt, had only been down a few years from the Big Smoke. Went from medium-sized fish in a festering huge swamp, to thinking they were all that and more by the sea in the West Country. They aimed to take the South West country bumpkin chavs in town for everything. But, they hadn't heard of Jimmy, his history overseas, or his friends in the gangs of Bristol and Cardiff — why would they? They could tell by his ways though, there was something about him, and wanted it easy. So they had left him alone — for a while.

Now though. They'd gotten greedy. Decided to test the boundaries.

They thought: We're from London. The fucks wouldn't know what hit them. Ominous looking he might be, with a look like he could have played a hardman back in London. But Jimi wasn't...was he. Just another South West straw chewing, cider guzzlin' farmhand like the rest...surely. About time he knew his place and fell into line with the rest.

'No one plays here. Except me 'n the girls. Ain't nothing gonna change that. Nothing you can do about it...'

He reached over the bar, grabbed the ball-pein hammer.

'CRACK' it went on the old wooden bar top. 'CRACK. CRACK' and they jumped at the repeat.

'Now get the fuck...in case you haven't heard. I'm

close to mourning.'

'We'll be back...'

'Yes, back,' The Echo said.

'Back in black,' Last Orders finished and giggled to himself.

'Shut the door behind you,' Jimi said.

A few moments later Tammy re-emerged... Betty's *points* came slowly after, the rest of her followed.

'How's about a three-way pick me up?' one said.

They all went outback.

Three

SAND POINT WAS HIS PLACE. He didn't usually let the emotions run free. Not anywhere but there. He'd spent every Sunday on that peninsular, thinking about his estranged son. He hadn't really spent any time with him. The boy's mother thought he was a bad influence. So, The Point, looking out from the rocky outcrop is where he imagined what could have been: taking him on as an apprentice, showing him the ropes. Drinking, smoking, building shit and bashing heads together.

It was an alternate existence.

It was his therapy. Lost in the sea breeze and found in the release of the waves.

He'd heard the boy had gotten into University, a college or something, God knows what he was working at now. Probably a desk jockey. Never gonna do a hard day's graft in his life.

The sun started to come down. A lone boat sailed past. The Universe seemed to stop, take stock, waiting before the darkness fell again.

He wouldn't budge on letting that lad, Matt, play his stage. The cockney-cocks would bring it on. Let them try.

In front, a rabbit dug its hole. And a butterfly, up past its bedtime, stopped on a blade of grass by his feet. A crow chased a seagull off a snail and the waves crashed on, relentless.

Jimi stood up, breathed it all in.

***

As he walked over the crest and looked down at the sand-covered car park he saw three shadows by his Transit van. If this place was lost to him. And wasn't sacred anymore. Nowhere would be.

There was going to have to be change.

The town would feel the shift. Like when he arrived and played that first power chord.

There was no going back.

***

The sparks flew as he drove. The punctured wheels didn't hold him back. He had momentum — somewhere to be.

It was about to kick off.

Matt stood expectantly with his brothers outside The Hell's Belles, a guitar case in hand. Jimi barged past all four as the place erupted and roared. Welcoming him home.

The brothers weren't getting in.

The bar cheered more as Jimi approached the stage. They knew his loss — this set was for him.

He picked up his case from the foot of the stage and plugged the jack lead, a catalyst for what was to come, straight in. The Gibson SG was light but it was weighed with the responsibility that night. Like a heavy full black cloud, lightning about to strike.

Letting the feedback build, the glasses rattled and the eardrums ached. Jimi stroked the devil-like horns to his instrument. It throbbed, the whole damn place did now too. The town was lost of any remnant of civility that had once clung on.

The eyes watched him eagerly, like looking up at Krakatoa from a beach hut below — the heat was about to come down on all of them. His guitar was the hammer pushing the keystone out of a bridge that held them all up.

Then he opened.

Everything was in that first chord. That song held it all; where he'd been, and where they were all headed.

They were on a Highway To Hell.

Four shadows peered through the condensation from outside.

They left before the chorus.

***

'Best ever set, Jimi,' she said and kissed him on a cheek.

'Best ever,' the other said, and kissed him on the lips.

'Girls… I think we better hold up a while. See how it pans out. Don't want either of you hurt on account of this.'

'Why not, cwtch up. It'll be our pleasure,' Betty said, winking and pulling shoulders and arms together.

Tammy nodded, poured them all a double.

They settled in for the night. The walls still groaned, but the place had emptied. The punters all gone. Only their sweat remained, dripping like salted treacle from the ceiling.

They looked out at the streetlamps shining across wet cobbles. Their lights bounced and shone into the bar. It was a sombre, uneasy tone.

They wondered what was next: How long before a reaction from those brothers?

He got out his phone. With a few clicks, he moved some names to Speed Dial. He didn't want to show weakness; to have to call *them*. But he wanted to be prepared.

If he did call or message, he knew they'd love it. To ride over and chase some London wankers out of 'Dodge City'.

Four

YEARS AGO, THEY'D ALL MET when Tammy used to grind the poles at the Big City Cat Club. She was even blonder then, it was in her contract — company's orders. Betty worked the bar, her hair just as blonde. Although, black as a raven underneath it. Both did hand-jobs outback for cash, making up for the tips that went to the miss-management.

Once, some city idiots were hassling them. Jimi was just minding his business, drinking off the absent family that grew ever distant with each drop and funeral he didn't attend. The backdrop of T&A was a nice to have ambience, he wasn't paying that close an attention.

Until the boys started getting rough with Tammy and the other girls. Betty crashed open the hatch and went over — barked at them to leave. Had one in an arm lock.

Jimi was impressed.

The three of them didn't know it, but she got her future job as his barmaid right then. And on twice the pay, without the punter gropes too. There were other perks too. She'd started Jimi's J. T. Trousersnake nickname. And it was a modest approximation.

Betty lost her grip, got slapped, was shoved, and pushed aside, like a rag doll.

They tried to drag Tammy behind a curtain.

Jimi intervened.

The boy's stag do was one to remember. They could drink as much as they liked but wouldn't forget being taken out two at a time in headlocks. Or those heavy 8ft solid doors cracked opened with their heads.

The bouncers giggled.

The police were outside laughing too. Waiting, letting Jimi enjoy doing their hard work. They nodded to Jimi. He'd fixed a roof or two for them and they were on his side. Knew he had honour, of sorts.

Jimi and the girls cut their losses, leaving emotional anchors and pimps behind. They pooled resources, bought a run-down bar on the coast, and never looked back.

Damaged souls, ostriches with heads in Weston's sands...

Now, they were family.

Cash Converters supplied the guitars, mic, and amp. He played on the street outside to get them in. It was never less than full every night from then on. And the rest, they say, is history.

***

Jack had never met his father, Jimi, but had turned out pretty much just like him. Much to his mother's disappointment. She was worried it was in his genes, programmed at conception...unavoidable.

He was smart. Proffered using his hands though. He'd got through college, got a certificate. Still, he wanted to use those hands more than the potential between his ears. He seemed destined to use those shovels at the ends of his arms to create...and when needed, to destroy.

His mother never spoke of his father. Other than to make his birthday a *nothing* event. Each year she'd sabotage his emotions and expectation, in commemoration of the fact his father apparently left a day before his first one.

'Can I see friends?'

'I'm workin'. Tin of beans in the cupboard. Bit of cereal left if you get stuck,' she'd say. That was when he was five. When he got older the conditioned dread each year was enough to appease her resentment, of him being from Jimi's seed. And from Jimi not being there, and her being stuck with the boy — rejected.

He only asked about his dad a handful of times, 'What does he do?'

'A builder, criminal, probably in jail.'

He knew it was a lie. Felt it. If he was all those things he would still be around with his skanky mother. No, he knew his father was meant for better things. Probably had some lame arsed, well-paid desk jockey gig in the city — all the things she pushed him to do.

Jack left it well alone… Knew he wasn't good enough for his father; like his mother. His confidence had been shot from birth — he accepted his fate.

***

'I might change my name,' Tammy said.

All three of them were up on barstools, on shots of JD, and gazing at the mirror behind the bar for answers that hadn't come yet.

'What?' Jimi asked.

'Yeah, why pet?' Betty whispered.

None of them shifted their gaze.

'Carol, Caity… Something with a C… Just Cat maybe.'

'Why?' Jimi said

'Why?' Betty echoed.

'We'd be JCB then wouldn't we. Like the diggers.'

'I've dug us into a right hole here that's for sure…' he smirked, looked around at them both, 'Tammy's perfect… Don't change a damn thing. The fucking digger company should change its name instead. In honour of one of the toughest, hottest landladies there is.'

'Aww… thanks, J. Who's the other?'

'Only one…sitting there hun. Sitting right there.'

All three laughed.

The answer had arrived.

It was going to be alright. As long as they were together. They'd be ok. And had what they needed…

Five

MIKEY WAS THE FIRST to turn up. Lanky sod, and ex-plumber. Used to work in the Navy in submarines. Could still hold his breath for two minutes and that was after smoking Marlboro for most of his life.

Jimi said, 'Alright there, Mikey? Pint of Fosters is it? Or have you stopped with that watered-down shite? And welcome to Crazy Town. A population of fucked up dropouts. And you?'

'I'll have a dose of whatever you're havin', then you can let me in on what you got going on here...' he said, just as Betty rounded the corner and his eyes damn near popped out. If his throat was dry before. He was drooling now. 'Make it a fucking double, Jimi,' as tammy appeared too closely after, pulling a tightly fitting sweater over her head, and a bulging bra. 'That bra is some kind of engineering masterpiece.'

'Sure is. Here's a triple.' Jimi said. And poured it. 'Let's wait for the others before the lowdown, don't wanna have to repeat myself.'

'What? Who else is turning up? No, you haven't called...?' He joked, 'hope you're well-stocked. This fucking town ain't big enough to hold them too.'

Next up: Stevie arrived with a ring of the bell above the door. A real engineer by trade, he could fix anything. Car, bike, train, or plane. He held a dark wisdom in the silence he left between sentences. Always wore black. He walked straight in and took a stool at the bar. Didn't say a thing.

'JD for him too...make it large,' Jimi said.

No one moved, waiting for the time to speak.

Bringing them together and the last to arrive, was Brian. A big bastard. Fucker worked back of house, on the computers, fiddling the books. Though to look at him you'd have thought he was a general labourer. His mouth was as blunt as his appearance.

'What's missing here bitches?' He said, addressing Jimi, Mike, and Steve, as he walked up to the bar and pointed at his open palm.

'I wanna say your limp dick, that you've been tugging at since lunchtime. I'll pour you a Gold anyhow,' Betty said, without knowing him.

'You've balls up top and going on. Jimi always was good at picking them. Well fucking balanced brains and rack.'

Tammy looked on, real protective. Jimi gave her the nod. It was ok. They all were closer than family too, despite Brian's slack mouth.

Brian started, 'Ice in cider me lover… Now, Jimi, what's all this shit about some fuckers wanting to draw their last breaths?'

They smoked.

They drank.

When their smoke was halfway up the room, the girls pulled out the drawers under the stage. There they were. His favourite claw hammer, a pickaxe handle, an array of smaller hammers, knives, a sword, and the Gibson SG. There was also an Epiphone Dot. It had a bluesy rattle and hum that he just loved after a couple of pints.

Jimi got up, did a couple of ACDC tracks. Then Brian played some Wonderstuff with the semi. It was a little softer than the walls were used to, but he made it work. It rocked the place, not the same, but it was good.

They were all bound together.

The neighbours didn't complain.

They never did.

***

Jack knew where to go, who to hit and how hard to get noticed in South London, to find a potential new employer.

He went down the Black Sheep in Oval. Hit some latte-sipping hipster spark out that was being too loud over the footy on the big screen in there. Talking about his window box veg patch or some shit like that...

Sure enough, he was noticed by the powers that be.

'Give that boy a free bar for the night! Take a seat,' a voice came at half time.

'Ok, sir.'

'Don't mind me calling you boy do you?'

'I know who you are, Mr Ballard. You can rightly call me whatever you like,' he said and wiped the blood from his knuckles.

'Take a seat then, CUNT,' and in a turn, the bald-headed once civil old man turned savage, and he was just that: a savage beast. 'Seen you about, son. Didn't realise you were on our side. Thought you were just a badly dressed civilian — like the rest.'

'I'm a grafter.'

'Like your father?'

'Never met him.'

'Often better off. Harder without. Softer with,' Max Ballard said. That's unless your father was anything like mine.'

'Everyone knows he was God on these streets, Mr Ballard.'

'You don't need to stroke my weasel any more, son. You got my attention. The old man did his time, worked hard. Had a following. Was a hard-hitting bastard behind closed doors with me and what was left of her indoors too,' he turned his head and turned his right ear down to reveal a scar.

Jack had heard the story. He knew Max had really done that to himself, in prison. He'd pleaded insanity and started hacking off his own ear with the cap of a Biro his solicitor had left on the table. He didn't know if it was a test by Max, laying on a lie. Knowing everyone and the boy would know the true story — maybe he wanted to know if he could trust him. See if he wasn't just gonna tell Max what he wanted to hear all the time — if they moved forward together.

'Madness of prison did that, Max. Sorry, Mr Ballard. And I heard your dad was solid. Never hurt any women or children. Almost as much as you.'

Max stared. He saw himself in the boy. The absent father — god he hated them. It would make this easy. 'I see big things ahead, son… Don't mind me calling you that, do you?'

'It fits,' said Jack.

And with that, he was to do Ballard's will — to do unto others, that you would never wish upon yourself. But no women or children. Like that, Jack had joined the South Side Cricketers. They didn't play the game, had a reputation with bats and balls though. And it wasn't the kind of club you could opt out of either.

***

'I think we should head in for the night,' Tammy said, lifting her head from the table at 3am.

'Long day tomorrow,' Stevie agreed.

Brian was already well gone and snoring on a bench at the side.

'Tomorrow, we hit the town. See what all this fuss is about,' Mikey said.

'Rip it a fucking new one,' Brian snorted from his sleep.

'Cheers lads,' Jimi said, 'The Brothers normally hit the slots for a skim off the profits at about two. So, you can get a decent kip 'till then.'

He took the girls upstairs as the lads watched their hourglass curves, arms around Jimi's waist, disappear through the doors together. They all smiled.

'He's done alright has Jimi,' said Mikey.

'Deserves it, all that happened to him,' Stevie added.

'We'll make it right…' Brian grunted, farting like a walrus, then snored on.

Six

THE CREW WOKE EARLY. Left Jimi to sleep, with more than his ample share of bosom for a pillow and helped themselves to a hair of the dog from behind the bar, before walking the promenade.

'Donkey ride later?' Mikey grinned as they strolled ahead with skulls full of post-hang-over euphoria.

'Aye, why not,' Stevie said, smiling at the sun as it fought the clouds for space in the sky.

'After...a chip stottie,' Brain added. 'If, these South-Western hillbillies have such a thing.'

Like a Banksy makeover of a Jack Vettriano painting: they walked across the sand flats. Three working-class heroes, matadors, on their way to the big bullfight.

They grabbed a tray of chips each from a cafe's hatch then crossed the road in front of the Grand Pier. The row of seafront shops and arcades looked shutdown, a sorry state, but they were open alright.

'Someone's been draining the life from this place...' Stevie said.

'For too long,' Mikey went.

'Let's get this shit over with — I want a burger,' Brian stated, speaking from his gut. He was always 'hangry'. A few more steps along and a seagull went for one of his chips. He punched hard with a free hand. It flew with the impact, not free will, and crashed into a nearby wall. As the bird twitched awkwardly, a nearby child cried out at the impact. Both bird and child stunned.

Mikey and Stevie mouthed an apology to the young mother, dressed only in only a pair of tracky bottoms and a bra top as she dragged the wailing toddler off towards the

Shopping Centre.

'Not so bad a view, sometimes,' Mikey quipped, and they marched on.

'You and me got different tastes, man,' Stevie said, shook his head and lit a Marlboro Red.

'Just the hangover horn talking. Take no notice. He'd bang a damp drainpipe right now,' Brian said and they laughed hard.

The other two took out Marlboro Lights and they lit up too.

The Weston-Cashino had a named pretension it would never live up to. It was a slot penny dive, and a hole. The deprived resorts were full of them up and down the country. How they paid rent let alone, gangsters, loan sharks and protection rackets they just couldn't figure out.

Rod Stewart was coming from the place next door: *Whole Slot of Luck*. And *Simply The Best* by Tina was flooding in from 'Lucky Lucky', next to that. Feel-good songs from an age gone by. Now, mere anthems to steal from pension books and to idle away time from teens in places like this.

'First thing we change — the tunes!' Brian said. As blunt as a sledgehammer.

'Can see how Jimi found his niche here. Fuck me...' said Mikey.

A car drove past playing Phil Collins.

'Fuck. This. Place,' Brian barked a staccato. Grabbing his head and ears that throbbed in protest.

They went into the first one. Took a perch on separate rows. Waiting for the proverbial bulls to show face, so they could dangle a red rag. And lance them hard.

***

When Mandy, Jack's mum, heard he'd joined the South Bank

Cricketers, from the Black Sheep pub, she was scared. Then, she heard Max Ballard had personally taken an interest, and she shook and cried through the night. So, when they told her on her next time in the pub, that they'd sent him to Weston-fucking-super-Mare — she was terrified.

She thought: What if he met his father? They'd end up fighting over the same tramp-girl in a bar or something. Without knowing who they were. That they were bound in blood. Even worse, they'd end up friends... and even closer.

And with that, Mandy could lose it all... Including him; their son. Damn it, he was her emotional punch bag. Something to channel and focus the resentment through. Someone to blame other than herself.

She needed him back. He had more college work to do. He had to get a decent job, so he didn't turn out like *him*. Someone has to pay the bills.

Fuck, he had already turned out worse.

His dad had been a builder, hung round with the gangs, got in favour for a few odd jobs with them. Never overstepped the law though. Ended up doing an odd bit of headbanging here and there, nothing major.

Damn it. Jack had skipped the building part. Gone full gangster.

Seven

JACK'S TRAIN RATTLED ALONG. He'd have read a book, but that life was behind him.

By Swindon, it felt like the point of no return. By Bristol, fuck, he might as well of be on a rocket to the moon... Then, the conductor started reeling off names he'd never heard of. They sounded like insults or nicknames for crooked priests: Bedminster, Nailsea, Backwell... Worle. What's coming next? He thought... 'Bend-overs-Ville'.

Max Ballard, his new boss, had told him there was some small town stubborn local, giving it some. Being awkward. Not playing the game. He'd sent the brothers over there to take it easy, away from the big smoke, breathe in the sea air. And to get some easy pickings from the junkies, slots, and wanna-be dealers. It wasn't London, it'd be child's play — except for this guy that was giving them shit... He wanted the heat to die down after their last job in London had gone bad. Another reason to send them South Westerly. And another reason why they couldn't get too hands-on and heavy with it. That's where Jack would come in.

Jack was nervous.

Ballard had said he didn't want those brothers pushing too hard. They were in enough trouble as it was. Things might go South if the local police joined the dots, talked to the London coppers. The Brothers easily got carried away. Loved their work too much — it's what stirred up the heat around them. Overzealous shaking down of a rival. Fuck they were still pulling bits of him out of the Thames. The bits they got bored pushing into the wood chipper.

So, it was down to Jack.

'Prime opportunity m' boy,' Ballard had said. 'You're unknown. They...can only scare this guy a little. You...can go further. Will...go further. Anonymous. No history. Off the fucking radar.'

Jack had listened hard. It was his big break.

'That's what it is, boy. Your big break. Prove yourself over there. And I'll welcome you back. When the Brothers come home, with you — there's a top spot waiting for you.'

***

A shape peered in through the bar window behind the black rain. First, she thought it was Jimi. That he'd finished with Betty upstairs. They'd been making the lights shake in the bar with their banging off and on for an hour. She looked up at the ceiling as the lights dimmed and vibrated — they were still at it alright.

She smiled for them.

The shape at the window wasn't one of the Brothers. Too stocky. Literally a younger ghost of Jimi. It tapped at the window, and again. Then it wrote 'are you open' into the rain on the pane.

She went over and replied 'not today' in the condensation.

As if on cue, and in sync, they lifted a cig up to each of their lips. Then came a lighter. Her's a Betty Page clipper. His a matt black Zippo. They went to spark up either side of the glass. Tammy's lit up. The shadow's flame failed. The rain won. A heavy drop fell from the window frame above and snapped his Marlboro in two. The soggy half dangled, then dropped as if in slow motion, to the cobbles below.

He made a sad clown face and shrugged.

And her heart melted.

He was in...

When Jimi rolled from the bed, he took each step slowly. One at a time. Contemplating what lay ahead. Looking down at Betty, she was still beaming in her sleep. From the hangover sex with an added lie in on top. Tammy had agreed to stand watch downstairs — as long as there was some 'afternoon delight' as promised.

He could barely piss straight. God damn, she was good. On his second stream, he heard voices downstairs, shook, and straightened up...

He grabbed the claw hammer from under the bed. Picked up a sleeveless t-shirt and ripped jeans.

He opened the door to the bar ajar, slowly cracking it open.

This would be quick.

'What's this, another rooster in the henhouse?' He said. Realising the shape at the bar was something new, not one of the Brothers. 'We said no one...' he whispered in her ear from behind. And he shelved the hammer.

'Thought it was you at first,' she replied.

'Don't see it,' he said, loud enough for him to hear. Jimi's self-image was close to Bon Scott and Brian Johnson from ACDC depending on how he felt at the time. When he was younger it was always Bon, now, mainly Brian. In reality, he was more Ray Winston in Sexy Beast.

The lad looked more Marc Bolan to Jimi, with a buzz cut.

The lad talked and so did Jimi. They were half a meter away on the better side of the bar. They started getting into who was the best singer of *this* band, and *that* band, alive or dead. And which guitar solo should have been longer, and which shorter. She stood up when they started on the 27ers club. And how they could form a supergroup from dead rock stars. She went upstairs to join Betty. She was happy he had connected, someone new to talk the ears off about rocking out.

A moment later the lad looked up at the flickering lights. 'Didn't realise we were that close to the station.'

The lights started to shake.

'We're not,' Jimi said, smiled and left it at that.

A second later Jack's penny dropped and they laughed and got out the JD.

***

It wasn't easy finding his van keys. Jack looked everywhere. Behind the bar. In the till. In Jimi's pockets... for fuck sake. They weren't upstairs, surely they weren't in the ignition. He couldn't risk it. She could be down any second, and with whoever was shaking that ceiling with her.

He'd laced Jimi's drink. Waited.

Seems Jimi had a huge bladder or was dehydrated — it took ages for the right time to drop the pill. He was worried Jimi had sensed his impatience at something a few times. Jack masked over it by asking him about music or guitars. It was an easy-play distraction. Like asking the Geography teacher about trains...so he would rabble on at length rather than teaching class. There was a flip side to that in retrospect, looking back at those school days. He had no more interest in hearing about the fucking Flying Scotsman than he did oxbow lakes or longshore drift.

He dug guitars though and this taste in music they had. With Jimi, he actually gave a shit — the guy was solid. Straight up. Shame Jack had to fuck him up.

He decided he had to just move. He'd hotwire the sodding van if need be. Dragging Jimi's mass across the bar floor he noticed a tattoo. Looked like it said: Mandy. His mother's name. Well, what the fuck? He thought. A happy coincidence. The sight of it, even with the scar cut through might be all he needed. To pretend this stranger, who he liked, was actually an arsehole who deserved what was coming.

From then on he'd try to blank him out, and just see *her*. It would make what he had to do a whole lot easier.

The van was open and keys in the ignition. Cocky bastard, he thought.

He dumped Jimi through the side and slid it shut. Sure that the familiar noise would rouse the girl and whoever else was with her. He grabbed his bag of tricks that he'd stuffed down the side lane and pulled a face at seeing the recent new bling tyres and alloys…

What a pimped-up piece of shit this is, he thought.

He put some addresses in his phone. Then, drove off towards Bristol Suspension Bridge.

Eight

J ACK CHECKED HIS ZIPPO WORKED. All good. And, that the lighter fluid tin had enough for the job. He finished tying Jimi up with the Bungee rope and lay him on the floor. Then he sat on a log facing him.

He thought: this is it, no going back. You liked this guy more than Max in the few words you shared together. You sure this is the career path?

The woods about them were alive with nature. Birds, rustling from bushes, distant pops of shotguns. This was the life.

He took out a quarter bottle of scotch.

Jimi murmured, almost coming to.

Yes, he thought... And it's time...to finish the interview.

'Want a drop?' he said to the heap on the floor.

Jimi just glared. Then he softened back a shade, to simple a stare. The boy's presence was both a comfort and disappointment.

Damn it he liked the kid why'd he have to be siding with those cockney twats...

'I thought you were okay kid,' and some spit fell as he spoke. 'I'll take a swig. Guess I'm gonna need it.'

Jack's confidence waned; Jimi grew more lucid. His words touched him. He couldn't hold eye contact as he bent down and poured the bottle into Jimi's mouth.

'You know I'm just a fucking builder. I know my fair share of heavy gang lads. I ain't one though.'

'That so,' Jack said to the mud on his shoes.

'They'd be the first to admit it...'

'How you end up here then?'

'Cos I wouldn't let some jumped up prick play my stage… It's for me an' the girls — end of.'

'Might seem a bit of an overreaction then?'

'Could say that. My pals won't see it that way though. They'll come down hard on the cockney pricks. It's already the fucking Wild West. You and your London lot aren't made for this. If you think a single builder gets this much going, imagine what the rest are like.'

'Not much good at begging are you,' and Jack looked on as Jimi's eyes faded again.

Jack took a different bottle from his bag, the one that wasn't spiked. He unscrewed the top and took a long hard swig.

A crow landed on a branch above Jimi's body as the light finished fading to night. A beautiful bird. Purest black. Builders v gangsters, what the fuck? He pondered. The crow flew down to Jimi's face, pecked at the tainted ground by his mouth then keeled over.

Jack cried.

He couldn't remember when he had last, or if he would again.

Something in the cosmos was shifting.

He closed his eyes and imagined an alternate reality: where his dad was a straight-up as this guy on the floor. They played guitar together and drank like bastards — chasing girls. Then they'd sit and watch the sunset over the sands. No harm done, no one hurt — unless some London prick touched one of the girls.

Jack opened his eyes, wiped them dry and got to business.

He looked at the carved-up tattoo of a girl's name as he lifted him into the van.

And then it happened, the next time.

He cried.

**

When Mikey, Stevie and Brian got back to The Hell's Belles, both girls looked a mixture of confused and scared.

'We don't know what's happened,' they muttered in unison. 'He seemed so... so...well, like him. They were just getting... y' know, along.'

'What the fucking-fuck,' Brian started. He wasn't much for sensitivity. 'You bitches lost

Jimi? Fuck. The only fucking fucker who fucking loses fucking Jimi... Is... fucking Jimi. FUCKKKK!'

They both looked just as scared but more perplexed as the words tumbled out of Brian.

Stevie calmly asked what had happened and told Brian to take a load off. Mikey shook and paced about, in the background, with his pent-up energy. Like a wrestler waiting to be tagged to go into the ring.

Brian went into his combat trouser pockets and emptied the contents: a Stanley knife, hammer, rolly tin filled with weed and skins, a wrap of speed, some sandpaper, a carpenters glove with reinforced knuckles, a folded prozzie flyer he'd found on a phone box in town and a biro. And...a Ned's Atomic Dustbin cd, some industrial tape, super glue, loose change, and a screwed-up fiver.

'Where was that fiver earlier you cheeky bastard,' Mikey said.

'You cunts earn more than me. You like treating me anyway,' he said and started to organise the contents of his pockets into two piles. 'Gonna need this...' he started the first pile, 'won't need this,' went the second.

By the end, the hammer and wrap of speed were in the 'needed pile', the rest laid to rest.

'Before you rip up the town like a Tasmanian

devil...' Stevie brought his calm to the situation. They were a good team. Better with Jimi too. 'His van's gone. We haven't a clue where he's at. Have we?'

Then Mikey chipped in, 'If you were gonna scare someone, where would it be? Or worse, do them over...?'

Stevie thought. It was his job: the thinker.

Mikey: the worrier.

Brian: the botherer.

'I guess a bridge. A building. A boat. This lad... was he local?

'No, don't think so. More London-ish. Must be. He's working with those fucking brothers isn't he.' Betty said.

'Think landmark then. Universally known. A high up jumping spot. For suicides and murders.'

'Severn Bridge!' they all said, in unison.

A spark of fire was lit under their seats. They jumped up.

Mikey necked a shot, and they all followed suit. Bang, bang, bang on the countertop.

'What was that shit you just gave me?' Brian asked.

'Absinthe,' Mikey said.

'Fair enough,' Brian said... 'Fair e-fuckin-nough.'

They packed up, tooled up and jumped up into Brian's van — a blacked-out transit with A-team red stripe.

The lads were in the back of the van on the wheel arches, the girls in the front. Brain asked them if they wanted to 'change gear' and 'touch his stick' a few times. Other than that they were fixed and focussed. In total silence. Except when Mikey squeaked one out.

'Sorry, IBS playing up. Shouldn't have had that shot.'

'We ain't stopping. There's a bucket back there,' Brian stated.

They motored hard, non-stop up the M5.

And went to the wrong bridge.

Nine

JACK LOOKED OVER THE EDGE of the decorator's cradle under the Suspension Bridge.

Jimi dangled a few feet beneath him, upside down.

He wasn't weakened. The world was against the man and he looked unshakeable.

'Sorry about this, Jimi. Just need to get a job. And this one, well, it has a slightly unconventional interview process.'

'It's alright, son… but you might not live to cash the first cheque.'

'Maybe, maybe.'

'What's a clever lad like you doing this shit for, with those morons? Get yourself a trade. Earn an honest crust.'

'Here you are. Dangling from Brunel's bridge, over the Avon Gorge. With lighter fluid dripped on you. And you're about to be set alight… You're gonna Bungee off of here and you won't know if the rope's gonna be long enough to dip you in and put the flames out. Or, if you'll just bounce up and down on fire for eternity… And you're picking now… Now, to be giving fucking careers advice. You've got some balls, Jimi. You really are quite something. I wish we'd met under different circumstances. I really do.'

'Not so bad yourself, son. Sometimes, it's the jobs where everyone's under the most pressure when you create the best bonds. The ones that last. I've had few like that,' he said, vein bulging as gravity dragged all of the blood to his head. He looked down, the whole 245 feet to the River Avon below. Then back up again. Still unphased.

'Where's the anger Jimi? Isn't this where you threaten to tear me a new one?'

'Liked your music taste. 'Sides, it is what it is...' he shrugged, upside down, 'And, you know what, you remind me of someone I never knew.'

'Doesn't make much sense... who?'

'My son.'

'Funny, my mam's called Mandy.' Jack said, pointing at the tattoo. Then flipped the Zippo, lit him up, and let him drop.

Their eyes met... Time slowed.

Jimi mouthed the word: Jack.

Jack's eyes widened, and so did Jimi's. Jack reached out for a boot but was too late. His heel slipped and his father was falling, on fire.

On the way down Jimi didn't see his past life. He didn't relive any of it. He saw a future. One that could have been. The lad and the girls. His bar: The Hell's Belles. And the boy doing a Bon Scott first half and him as Brian Johnson for the rest. The girls would play full sets alternate nights so they all got to enjoy each other. Who knows, maybe they'd all share more than the stage.

High Voltage Rock N Roll.

He smiled. He'd never been so happy.

***

Brian was the last of them back through the door of The Belles and forgot to lock up. 30 minutes later, the Brothers crashed in. Not as hesitant as last time they let their true feelings flow.

'So, when's he going to be on? And how much is in the register girls?'

Brian, Mikey, and Stevie stood up fast. But the girls were faster. Already there. Tammy pointed the claw hammer and Tammy had the ball pein.

'Ooh, nasty. I like it — you girlies play rough.'

'Where's he at?' Tammy snapped.

'You boy's dunno what you've opened here,' Mikey said.

'Yeah. you guys and girls don't know what you narrowly missed… cocky country bastards. For fuck sake. This is the big leagues — where from London don't you know,' The narrator said.

The girls started, then Mikey, Stevie and Brian joined in. They rolled about. Laughing. Pissing themselves.

'What tossers,' Brian said to them.

One of the Brothers went to put his hand into an inner pocket. Maybe for a gun. Maybe just to suggest it and scare them.

They didn't get a chance to see if it worked.

***

Some shadows appeared at the window, and they all turned. Then the door opened a little. Slowly a burnt forearm appeared, with blistering flesh and oozing pain.

The Brothers looked shocked.

Everyone else froze.

'All under control, girls, I see,' Jimi said, emerging and smiling. Hard as ever.

The brother's jaws dropped…

Then in walked Jack — bold a brass. Had Jimi's side. They both had crowbars. Jimi spun his then pointed it at The Narrator. That's all it took. They knew the tide had shifted. The boy had fucked up. Changed colours. Taken the top spot for most hated in Weston, now above Jimi.

'This won't end here,' The Narrator said glaring at Jack, then Jimi, then back to Jack on the way out.

'Won't end,' went The Echo.

'You just lost the best job you never had,' Last Orders said.

'What can I say, boys… Took a better offer,' Jack said and looked at his dad.

They laughed. Locked the door and poured a drink.

'What the fuck?' Brian started.

'Long story, lads. And I'm not sure you'd believe it anyhow. Let's just say I've done a bit of long hard thinking…and bridge swinging…on fire.'

'Can see that,' Betty said, 'let's get you seen to.'

'Aye, we'll get that arm bandaged too,' Tammy added, smiling.

'We're gonna need more help,' Stevie said.

'Too right,' Jimi agreed.

'What's the last big job you worked on?' Mikey said, to everyone.

Jimi started: '10,000 sq ft office block in Worle. Had loads of crews on it. Chippies, sparkies, plumbers… came from all over. Had the best of local lads on it too — good joiners. Was some tough Poles and Geordie lads there, worked like dogs. Strong. Drank and worked like bastards.'

'Think they'd be up for it? The London lot will send for reinforcements. Maybe we should reach out now too… Be prepared.'

'Already have. Already have,' Jimi said.

'Who, how many of them?' Mikey asked.

'All of them.'

'And they're coming?' Mikey asked.

'With a free bar on offer. And some cockney twats throwing their weight around…yeah, they'll come… Now, Jack. What's this Max Ballard like? Say it again, real slowly, so everyone here can take it in.'

'Savage. Real savage,' Jack said.

'Riff raff,' Jimi said and picked up his SG and headed

for the stage.

Betty dangled some bandages expectantly, knowing she was gonna have to wait to play nurse...

'It can wait. Me an' the boy gonna christen the stage first.' And Jimi held up the black Epiphone Dot for Jack.

***

Max thought hard, how had he got this so wrong? He never got anything wrong — he was fucking god. The heat was closing in on them after the brothers' indiscretion with the body parts under London Bridge. They needed to sort this Weston-super-Shitstorm out... And they'd need to play a shade softer than usual.

'Lads, pack your bags. You're taking a break. And leave the tools behind.'

A little holiday by the sea was just what they needed. A fists, heads and knees job only. Then they could catch some rays, play the slots, have a donkey ride.

***

'Better stock up, get some Newcy Brown in for the Geordies,' Jimi thought out loud.

'Vodka for the Polish lot,' Stevie added.

'Whiskey, Guinness and everything else for the Irish,' Jack said.

'Not wrong there... Restock of JD too... You sticking to the Absinthe then Mikey?' he looked around but couldn't see him. 'Hang on, where is he now?' Jimi looked at Mikey and co.

'In the shitter. IBS playing up. Don't think he'll be touching the green crap again...just get him some Fosters in. Brian said, not even looking up.

The police turned up next. Two of them, plodding along. Not exactly the dynamic duo. More a pair of half stoned koalas in uniform. Uninvited guests, nonetheless.

'What the hell happened to your arm, Jimi? One said looking at the bandage.

'Well, the boy here tied me up, set fire to me and chucked me off the Clifton Suspension Bridge.'

They laughed. 'Somehow I doubt that. Or one of you wouldn't be still stood here!'

'Chip fat,' Jim said.

'That's less likely than your first answer. Everyone knows where you go for your fish suppers — anyway… Where's B.A.?'

'What? said Jimi.

'Fucking A-Team van outside's been on double yellows all night.'

'Brian ran,' he hated getting a ticket or clamp. Sods to get off.

'Betty… Betty Jardin isn't it?' The other one said looking at her, 'Knee'd the manager of the City Cat Club in the balls and made off with a month's worth in tips wasn't it?'

'I guess,' Betty winked, stroking her pitch-black silky hair.

'Good on you. Hair looks better natural too. What's it with that guy insisting the girls bleach it all out.'

'Not just the heads either. Muffs 'n arseholes too.' Tammy interrupted. Matter of fact. From experience.

'Suppose you've had a whiff of something?' Jimi came out with it. They were all thinking it… That the coppers were treading water with the small talk. Had something playing on their idle minds.

'Don't like those pricks from The Smoke any more than you do Jimi. We've run some checks… they've some pretty ugly connections though.'

'Me too,' Jimi Smiled, just as the local chippies and labourers from Bristol, Clevedon and Portishead walked in…

'Thatchers it is. And since it's a free bar. One for Jimi and 'is pals too.' The first one went.

The police laughed.

'You got this, Jimi. Haven't you? Hope so. Just don't play too rough on those soft Londoners.' They said, about turned and went to walk out.

'One for the road? Thirsty work doing sweet fuck all,' Jimi said to their backs.

'Oh, go one then,' and they about turned again, took off their hats and joined the rabble. 'If you lot's the posse, gonna chase them out a dodge. Guess we might as well take a load off — less paperwork. Cheers!' and they lifted their glasses. 'Sure you got enough lads though?'

'You can take that fucking ticket and clamp off 'n all!' Brian said carrying them and another round of drinks over. He put them down and they handed him a key for the camp.

Brian appeared a moment later with a crunched up ticket, unfolded it and passed it to Jack, 'Fucking jokers,' Brian said.

Jack read it out: 'I ain't gettin' on no plane fool!'

Ten

MORE GROUPS ARRIVED. And the place was heaving with half-cut sparkies, chippies, joiners, plumbers, and carpet fitters.

The girls took to the stage. This was Jimi's place. But he knew who was really in charge.

'Ladettes… lads and layabouts,' Tammy started. And looked straight at Brian.

He mouthed: 'fuck off' and grinned. He was a sucker for girl power. That, and she wasn't totally wrong…had to give 'em that one.

'Thanks for coming…' Betty added.

A wolf whistle was quickly subdued at the back, as Mikey had a word in the ear of someone that should've known better.

'There's a savage London wind coming. Some cock knockers from the Big Smoke think it's alright to come over here and chuck their weight around.'

A supportive cheer rose and echoed outside where a number had spilt out onto the cobbles. They were joined by locals. All wondering what the fuss was about — and why the sudden influx of white vans everywhere.

Some girls at the front. A mixture of electricians and decorators turned to shush the room down. Brian joined in with his hands, waving them down and it all quickly simmered. Everyone wanted to know what the deal was.

'The deal is… simple,' Tammy took over, 'keep them in check. Make them feel as unwelcome as you like… play as rough as you like, without getting burned or locked up. We're not villains like them. And we've got something else, we've got real lives back home to return to.'

'There's envelopes over there with Mikey for each crew. Get yours on the way out,' Jimi said, 'little missions, reccies and fact-finding… All good fun. And at the end of each day, we'll see you at the bar. Back here for some fun. Rock N' Roll Damnation to them,' he shouted and made devil's horns with a fist.

***

'Bob and Margaret', were a team of *four* bespoke joiners from Bedminster in Bristol, none of which were called Bob or Margaret. They made industrial furniture out of rubbish they found in skips, upcycled it in their garage and sold it to office fit-out companies for a huge profit. They'd inexpensive tastes, no responsibilities; an easy life. Four middle-aged hipsters, they'd a slight paunch each, dungarees, sleeve tattoos, striped shirts, and a constant reefer on the go.

They opened their envelope, looked out to sea, and read it:

'Get shit. Throw shit. The Brothers park their Merc' at the front of Slots R Us. Reg is: CRICK 666.'

'Smoke da shit too,' one said doing an awful attempt at a Jamaican accent.

'Well looks like we're in for some muck spreading boys,' another said taking a toke.

They grinned, continuing to look out to sea; felt the slow serene embrace of the gange.

Sparked by the note and the weed influence. Pete, the oldest, pondered his childhood on the family farm. He remembered sitting on his father's knee in the tractors and combines, swilling out the pigs, late nights, and early mornings — it was bliss. Until the swine flu landed. His dad drank through it but not out of it… Pete shook his head, keeping the serenity intact. Refusing to let the memory of finding him in the hay shed, hanging from the beams. The sun caressed the sands in front of them, painting rainbows in the discarded pool of petrol or diesel left by the horse truck that had delivered the daily donkeys.

He smiled. Breathed. The beauty found in ugliness reminded him it was alright. Always another way of looking at it.

An old lady stopped with a much older, in dog years, Border Terrier. It looked at the four of them, panted, ate a leftover chip. Then it haunched up and assumed the position. It took the little dog five minutes to empty its guts. And a minute longer for the old lady to notice. She started rummaging in her trolley for something to bag it up...

'Bob & Margaret' all looked at each other.

'Let us do that for you, love,' and Pete stood, smiling, and patted her on the back. He rummaged in his pockets and found some Bonios he had for Fred, his Labrador at home. He gave the dog the biscuits, smiled again and took out a small bag from another pocket.

'Always have one,' he laughed to the others… Just in case.'

***

The Brothers left Slots R Us in a hurry.

Max had been on the blower and told them to play taxi. Some of the SBC (South Bank Cricketers) were getting a train across. And they couldn't be arsed with the two-minute walk from the station.

'What the fuck?' The Narrator said looking at the turd on the roof of the Merc'.

'...the fuck?' Echo said.

'Someone or something is gonna regret that,' Last

Orders said.

When they rounded the car there was a dog waste bin on its side. Then they turned to see the entire contents of the dog waste bin had been spread over the handles, windows, and doors.

Their temperature rose. Fuming.

The Narrator kneeled and punched the pavement.

A seagull landed on the roof. The flapping of its wings sent the lone turd rolling off with a thud. The bird squawked a laugh at them then disappeared. Chasing a shitty carrier bag down the seafront.

***

Jimi took a stroll. His ex-wife was threatened by his need for time alone, for headspace. Hell after Jack was born she was jealous of it. It was essential to his making, what brought him back together. When he was hurting, it was a purge. When happy, it was a glow.

The girls, Tammy, and Betty, knew it was a core part of Jimi being Jimi. The times when he went walkabout, sat on Sand Point looking out to sea, or at the end of the pier, reflecting on life — these were sacrosanct.

They loved him. He always came back to them. That was the good part, that and when did, he was carrying less worry. Until it all built up again.

He had a lot on his mind this time. Jack was in his life again. His ex would be stirred up at some point, if not already and would come to find him. And Max Ballard was sending a small army to do God knows what. Fuck knows what would happen if Max himself ever turned up; the Devil incarnate.

Above him the clouds were in turmoil; unsure what weather to bring. And below his feet, it seemed harder as his feet ground footprints into the freshly settled sand.

He'd got as far as Uphill, the next settlement along. He was headed for a ruined fort at the end of the 318 ft high peninsula by Brean Sands. Built to defend against Napoleonic invasion… he wondered what it'd be like against a load of wide boy cockney gangsters.

Yes, Jimi needed a stroll.

The fort had a bleak aspect. More like a prison. He was lucky, had kept hands clean so far. What he actually knew of prisons was from the others had been, and what he'd seen of Strangeways driving past when he did a job in Salford. Grotty depressing shit-hole that was at the time — industrial, bleak and grey. Jimi needed water, preferably the sea in his life. Manchester's trolley filled canals didn't cut it.

You can't beat the sounds of waves, that won't stop. No matter what its waters will wash, clean, and purify the soul.

I wonder if I'll get through this one with hands still clean, he thought.

He looked out at Steep Holm Island. With its almost vertical sides, lush green covering, leftover gun replacements and lookouts dating back to Roman times. Maybe me, the lads and lasses should take over that rock, he thought again, like pirates. And leave this shit-house world behind, start afresh. It was tempting. He saw another alternate future: the good life, easy livin', the sounds of wildlife, cut off from the outside. Except for occasional trips to shore to answer a call from the police, or someone in need, to dig them out of a hole. To bash some ugly heads together or fix a roof. He picked up his phone. Was about to call the girls, tell them his idea. Then, reality sank back in. That's what these strolls were also for. To see an infinity of possibilities, before reality hit back. To decide whether to grab on or slide back into the sludge of it all.

He stood up, walked back — slid right back in.

Eleven

MAX BALLARD LOOKED at the shards of glass sliced into his palm. He felt nothing. The rest of the pieces were on the table and the wooden floor beneath his chair. The punters in The Black Sheep had long since cleared a space around him. Before he'd destroyed the glass with the weight of his thoughts, he'd been emanating pure violence…like a stick of dynamite down to its last fraction of a fuse. Then it blew.

The pub about him froze, dust and smoke hung in the air. The TV reception stopped showing Newcastle being five down, playing away…then as the glass settled, it all started back up again. But, as if the world had now been turned to half volume for the benefit of Max Ballard's thoughts.

The manager had stopped the barmaids serving him. It was nerve-racking enough for him, as he tiptoed over every so often to douse the flames of Ballard's anger with expensive Japanese Whisky.

Not that he'd know. Ballard's 'slate' was endless.

Max had found his Zen by the 7th tumbler. By the 8th he'd picked the last bit of glass from his palm, putting it into the ashtray with a loud 'clink'. And then he lowered his arms to let gravity drip the last of the blood to come. Before the wounds hardened over.

Like life, he thought, the scars never really go away fully. Go away enough to move on eventually though — always. Left just a little more colourful than before, with a story to tell after.

Someone's Jack Russel Terrier ran over and lapped at the pool of his blood on the floorboards. He looked down, smiled, and beckoned the barman over.

'Bowl of water and some biscuits for the dog,' Max whispered in his trembling ear.

'Yes, sir,' he replied and scampered off, double-quick.

'Love dogs,' Max said to the back wall, 'obedient...know who's who and what's what. Bit of a turn in the hierarchy when we started picking up their shit though, admittedly. But still, little furry fuckers know who's in charge and who their masters are.'

He took another sip.

'You could learn a lot there, Jack. You see...' he said to the dog smiling up at him but imagining his latest boy-recruit gone awry in Weston, 'if only you were as aware of your place as this little namesake of yours here, Jacky-boy. We'd have been alright...wouldn't we...wouldn't we,' he repeated and gritted his jaw tight.

The pub and the dog's owner were getting nervous. For the dog. And them too.

Max bent down and picked up the small dog and put it on a knee. Stroking its ears back hard, it's eye's strained to see through the tightened skin. Despite this, they both looked a sort of happy. Then he held the dog by either side of its head. Looked deep into it. His palms leaving a bloody smear either side of its trembling little white face.

They were eye to eye.

The pub took an intake of breath. Held on to it. The dog whimpered a little in submission. Jack Russells never usually back down. Hardened ratters and badger baiters tools. Ballard's look had its will weakened immediately.

He smiled, put a finger in his drink and let the dog eagerly lick at the overpriced amber liquid.

Max walked out of the pub to go and pack his bag.

He had a bit of a drive ahead. Google said, 3hrs

24mins to Weston-super-Mare from Oval. Fuck that, he thought, he'd have the driver do it in 2hrs, or he'd lose a finger.

***

I.B.S. Building Contractors, from Portishead, were a team of five. Three men, two women. They had long since said goodbye to the founding directors. The ones with the surnames that had led to the unfortunate acronym in the company name. They'd stuck with it, could have rebranded… They had a reputation and that's what mattered. And also an unofficial tagline: 'getting shit done' — so it kind of fitted all round.

There were two Bobs in the crew. They sat on a bench with Dylan, Cherry and Karen standing. Twisting the envelope over and over in their hands, they passed it round in a three-way circle. A music-less game of pass the parcel where the prize benefit was uncertain.

They were all excited. And had taken Jimi's calling willingly, but also were well aware, any action on this little brown envelope's contents could land them in bother — up to their necks.

'Jimi said it, didn't he, play rough, or not too rough, summit like that,' Dylan started, 'we'll be okay — just a bit of tomfoolery…'

'Who talks like that man…tomfoolery… What the fuck?' Bob *one* said and Bob *two* snorted.

'Let's be havin' you, Jimi. How much shit are you gonna land us in with this one?' Karen said and picked the envelope from Cherry's hand. She talked and started to open it: 'Remember that client he introduced us too in Bristol… Way back now. Insisted on all those recycled scaffolding planks everywhere. Doors, tables, tops of cupboards — fuck me. Then they dried out two weeks out after we'd left. Air conditioning warped them something rotten. Fucking banana boats everywhere?'

'Well, good job we got the boards cheap. And still got paid for the labour,' Bob *two* said.

'Be glad when the damn industrial-chic crap is done with. Bring back minimalism,' Dylan said, 'now the envelope, what's it say? Put us out of our misery, Karen. For fuck's sake.'

She tore at the last bit of the flap eagerly, smiling. Then slowed to peep inside. The others were on the edge of their seats — and she loved it.

Then she read it out:

'BOOMSHACKALAKA, lads and lasses...

We've heard wind there's some heavies or London lightweights, however you wanna look at it, on the train. Due in at 3.45 this afternoon… I think they'll stand out. They were likely due a pick up from the Brothers. We had the stoners from Bedminster coat their car in shit… So, might be a while cleaning it up.

See if you can intercept them, say you're there to meet them. Get them drinking.
They won't be able to refuse you, girls, and Dylan. The Bob duo might have to hang back and do the paying…
Not so sweet on the eyes ;-)'

'Cheeky bastard,' Bob *one* went.

'Fairy muff,' Bob *two* conceded.

Jimi was right. Not hard to spot at all. It was sodding Summer-ish temperature-wise. And there they were. A hand full of plebs, looking out of place, long black coats, and holdalls. Looking lost, as if they'd just done a bank job but the getaway driver hadn't turned up.

The girls went over.

'We're to take you to The George and Dragon, lads...' Cherry said.

They didn't argue, ask who said so, or anything. Just nodded, picked up their holdalls and marched in a tidy line. Not saying a word. The two Bobs and Karen lead the way. Dylan and Cherry brought up the rear.

'Form a crocodile,' Bob *one* said at the front.

Cherry giggled at the back.

There wasn't a smirk or reaction anywhere in the middle. They just marched on like a robotic funeral possession.

The George and Dragon was a proper old boozer. A wood bar and a wooden rack above it with dusty glasses. The face of the Queen and Lady Di' on Toby Jugs. Wood chairs and wooden tables. And those wooden faced regulars varnished with a lifetime's bad choices. Its thick carpet stuck like a layer of half-dried chewing gum with each step. And the smoking ban had revealed a previously masked stench that could only be ignored after three pints, minimum.

Weston was the same as London in that respect. Full of these time capsule holes too — they'd be on familiar ground; fit right in.

Bob *two* ran ahead and ordered so they had drinks waiting at the bar: 'Five pints of pissy lager. Cheapest you've got. Dirty as you like. Hide a couple of nasty Tequilas in each of them too...'

'On the house, this time,' the barmaid winked, 'Jimi's slate.'

By the fourth round, they'd loosened up a bit. Speaking a little, asking about where they were staying. What the food was like. Their mobiles hadn't had the chance to rescue them with a call from the Brothers. Didn't help whenever they left a mobile unattended one of the girls switched it off. Or dipped it in a drink.

By the seventh round, one of the London lads was chundering outback. Using the porcelain Armitage Shanks phone to talk to God, Jesus and then resorted to: 'Max's not gonna like this'. He wiped the remnants of a half-digested cheap train sarnie, mixed with a gallon of Tequila and Fosters from his chin. Then, he fell backwards out the cubical onto his arse into the urinal.

When they were at double figures and suitably incapacitated. I.B.S Builders left them to it.

'Getting... Shit... Done!' Cherry said and they all did a mini high five before heading to the beach. It was still kind of early and they fancied a paddle, ice cream. Something to wash the taste of Foster from their mouths.

'We could have had anything...' Bob *one* said.

'Best not to raise suspicion,' Karen said.

'You're right though. Wish we'd had ours with the dirty Tequila spikes too,' Cherry finished. And they headed past the sign that said, 'Danger! Sinking sand and mud.' Made their way to the point where the sand met the sea. Where one force was perfectly in touch, influx, and dancing with another.

Like they all were.

Twelve

MAX HAD REACHED the Slough Junction, but his mind was already at the final destination. He imagined and played it over. Like a tape recording, each time he rolled it back it got more and more distorted, warped.

And he liked it.

His intentions needed honing, he knew that… The blade that was his darkest thoughts was focussed. But he was unsure; drive it home blunt or like a razor? To suffer or to be put to rest quickly? Such are the dilemmas of a hard-edged well-weathered London gangster that's been wronged. Was he perturbed? No, not anymore. He lived for this shit. A bit of revenge violence and suffering. Damn it was in his blood. He should have been born in a different era. He should have been a Viking.

'Turn the radio on, Jeeves,' Max said to his driver. Whose actual name was Danny.

Louis Armstrong was getting stuck into It's A Wonderful World. Max smiled, leant back, and got comfortable. He savoured the possibilities of differing horrors he might inflict. On Jimi, Jack… On Weston-bastard-Supermare. From the pits of his imagination, he would wreak havoc. Creating his masterpiece: Hell-on-Sea.

Then he reigned back in. Like a big cat at the edge of running water. He remembered the police had him and all the SBC (South Bank Cricketers) boys in their sights. It'll all be okay, he thought, he'd turn the place into the brawling, bashing, mashing self-destructing Wild West. Then, he'd get the fuck out and leave Jimi and Jack in a hole.

***

Worx 4 U Ltd. were generally referred to, in the trade, as Pricks n' Mortar and were half-drunk and fully stoned most of the time on building sites. Thing is, they were good lads outside of that, easy to get on with and they got stuff put up pretty quick. Usually, it stayed up... So, Jimi knew to have them on call. Reliably unreliable, clumsy, and yet, somewhat loyal. Like puppy Labradors.

On one job, they jumped in the van; usual 3.15pm clocking off time and revved the engine. They went to pull off, full of pride. Putting it in reverse by mistake, they totalled 'Mr and Mrs Pissed Off's' garden wall that they'd just finished. To be fair, and true to their reputation, they'd stayed until midnight; got it back up the same night. It was straighter and stronger too. A quick sobering up doused in shame did that. They might have hidden the client's cat, Henry, in the foundation; an unforeseen casualty of the wall mishap — but karma, of sorts, was restored.

In Weston, they were all in black Cargo trousers and white company logo t-shirts. One of them had Jimi's letter poking out a back pocket as they played the slots. They moved from an old Star Wars trench simulator to Operation Wolf to fire Uzis. They soon got to the *Outrun* driving game and that was it, distracted; loose change drained from them.

'I'm outta coin and beer,' Pete said.

'Me too... and I need a smoke,' said Sam.

'Hmm, aye me too,' went Willie and scratched at his balls.

They started fishing, poking around for more notes to cash in.

'Knew there was something we were meant to be doing,' Sam found Jimi's envelope,

and he held it out.

They all did a nervous half-laugh.

All three retreated from the distractions of superficial pleasure, and the flashing lights which had held them transfixed — like hypnotised budgies. Taking a bench outside, one of them started to read it out:

'I love you, guys, but you ain't half a clumsy, half-cut three-man wrecking ball at times... Can you just hang around Slot R Us — here's a fifty?'

'Already there, Mo Fo!' Willie said.

'It's the Brother's main place...one of their bases. Just play, drink, see what happens. And I'll see you back at the ranch.

Love, Jimi and The Girls'

They looked at each other in unison.

'Saaaweeet,' Pete said taking and smelling the fifty like it was a rose petal on forbidden girl's thigh, and walked straight back in.

The others followed. Hope, positivity, and energy. Almost skipping like young drunks to a free bar.

Two hours later they stumbled out. Smoke billowing out from behind them. They seemed quite calm, like sloths, meandering and stumbling casually out looking for chips.

Their work there was done.

Turned out the Street Fighter II game wasn't so good at absorbing Willie's pint of Cider and Black. Turbo Outrun was a little worse for wear too after Sam wouldn't give up his high score and got caught short. Pete had simply left his calling card in the toilets. They were barred from several boozers back home for the same reason. Too much fibre, not enough… They hadn't got to the bottom of it. He was a toilet terrorist. And for that reason Jimi made him use the public bogs during his stay.

Jimi knew, at some point, the guy was gonna blow. And that, at least, would be his gift to the Brothers. Anything else they broke, that'd be a bonus.

***

When Jimi got back, the front of the Belles was covered — an old school tar and feathering. But, less the tar, more cheap glue, and a plucked seagull. The naked body of which was nailed above the door like an old dripping glove.

'I kinda like it,' he said to Betty and Tammy who were stood outside.

It was in their eyes. They looked hesitant like they looked at a restored vintage Morris Minor about to go over a cliff edge…and they had no way of saving it. He could tell, there was more.

'That's not all,' Tammy said.

'You can probably tell by our eyes,' Betty said.

He turned slowly. His van was gone.

They'd left the alloys on the street as if holding the invisible body of his transit up. He laughed. Then, not so much. About turned, and walked away — he needed another rethink

***

Pitches & Hoes did groundworks, football, rugby grounds and occasionally a massive garden.

Usually, these urban oasis type spaces were found next to a swimming pool — nice work if you could get it and need a cool off when the client was away for a fortnight in

St Lucia whilst you completed the works. With a black VW T5 each and matching logoed-up jumpsuits, they looked like they were high-end security guards.

Jerry, John, and Andy: they were serious. Meticulous.

'Let's get this done,' Jerry said.

They hadn't sat since the initial briefing and gathering. They'd taken the envelope and walked the town; surveying, inspecting, weighing up the playing field.

Working their way past the barriers, real stealthily, they made a path to the end of Birnbeck Pier; officially closed to the public since 1998. A knowing nod to the guard and tourist kiosk was all it took — that, as though they were operating on some high-level official police business.

'Look at this beautiful old girl. A Victorian masterpiece. I hope they restore it,' Jerry said to the wind, 'Would make quite a setting for the final showdown, wouldn't it?'

The sun cut through a light sea fret; flared, dancing through the particles. Perfectly silhouetted; the shapes marched towards a battle plan. The pier creaked and groaned in agreement, as the three of them carried the weight of an entire army.

They stood staring out at Wales and opened Jimi's message:

'You three are rock solid. If no one else turns up, I'll be happy if you guys have, and you're reading this.

Now, the security firm that runs the CCTV for the police in town is pretty shit. But, it's pretty widespread and whether or not they're off asleep or out to lunch most the time is beside the point. When the police need to check on some shitty corner of town they seem to be able to get footage. Trust me, I know. Been caught, pants and

*head down a few times… Girls too, skirts up — if you
know what I mean?*

*Befriend, accost or whatever… Get us tapped into that
system. We're gonna need to know people's movements.
Tammy and Betty can monitor from base. They're like
Caesars already, running the show… True grit — war
commanders the pair. Gotta love 'em.'*

'No problem, Jimi son,' John said, his slight Geordie accent
coming through.

As efficient as a well-tuned machine, without
speaking much other than a concentrated word or two, they
went back to their vans. Black utility vests went on, with lots
of important-looking pockets. Then, to the print shop that
they'd spotted on their recce of the town. To print six logo
stickers: ELITE SECURITY SQUAD. Three for the front,
Three for the back. Perfectly sized to go over the existing
branding.

The rest was very quickly made history. Walking
straight into the security office, more of a Portakabin on the
outskirts, the half-asleep guards cowered instantly.
Shrinking, retreating like snails into their shells… The only
place they could go, and it wasn't far enough.

'Yes, sir, we'll redirect a copy of the feed,' one said.
Almost about to ask permission to breathe before and after
speaking.

'When we're done here. And these London clowns
have left town. We'll let you know…until then we'll be
watching them. And you!'

With that Jimi's new *Elite Security Squad* left — job
done; eyes in place. They could watch every part of town,
inside and out, like a fly on the wall.

**

Jimi was on a boat to the island: Steep Holm. It called him more and more. A walkabout wouldn't do it after they defaced The Belles and took his van: Rosie. He needed to feel the rhythm of the waves caress him. He needed to touch the hands of ancient war gods and come back fighting fit.

Inside, a voice said, screw this feuding — take over the whole island. Rebuild the inn. Rearm the fort. Man the observation post. In time, it'll all blow over and you can live the Good Life. Just you and your two Barbaras… Once a year you could hold a party, get them all back to reminisce. About the time they stood up to the wide boys.

The trawler let him off on a pebble beach and he alighted to the shingle stones, shin-deep in the waters.

'See ya in an hour or so?' The female skipper said, waved as then chugged and bobbed away.

'See you on the other side,' he said, pointing to the next bay along. It was marked with a big rock that looked like a calf bending to drink. He walked up and the stones massaged his feet through his sodden trainers. Natures embraced did the rest as gulls cried out, the wind whipped about the cliffs and the sea ushered him on.

Ancient looking steps lead up the sides of the hill and cliffs. An old inn used for centuries for thirsty fishermen stood lonely and roofless. Despite dilapidation, it still shone. Memories, dreams, of resting hard-working men and women, doused in illicit liquor. And their blood and toil marking every step he took. It was steeped through the old inn's walls when he reached its ruins.

He sat in the shell of the old drinking den. Took out a hip flask of JD. With each sip, the importance of history on the mark we leave on became more and more apparent. To roll over and become nothing. Or to stand up, maybe lose everything but be counted and to be remembered — so, have everything.

His muscles burned from the climb and his stomach did from the bourbon.

He needed to get back, he thought, he told them to stay locked up. He should be looking after the girls.

His phone went...

'Jimi, it's Betty,' Tammy cried, 'she's gone.'

Thirteen

A FORCE OF NATURE, MAX swept down the M4 like a hurricane. A torrent of anger and simmering rage.

Whilst he settled into the leather caress of the Merc's back seats, another turmoil was starting to bubble inside of him.

'Erh, Mr Ballard...'

'Yes, Danny.'

'That bacon sarnie we had from the burger van on the way out...'

'Prime cut of pig's flesh, son. Been going to Jason's Donnervan for years. What about it?'

Max's eyes tightened. As did his reluctant chauffeur's in the rear-view mirror. The penny dropped; both their sphincters simultaneously quivering. A bead of sweat ran down Ballard's forehead and he gripped the seat tight.

'Put a foot down, son.'

'It's to the floor, sir.'

'Then make like Fred Flintstone and put them through the floor and start running — before there's a serious fucking arsequake back here!'

Reading Services was usually something to avoid. Now, as they were both touching cloth, it was like a shining beacon. A welcoming busty hostess with open arms. They screeched into a disabled parking space upfront. Then, burst out racing, doors left open, car unlocked. Their legs and cheeks clenched together, as they raced, wobbling, like a couple of penguins to a fish banquet.

'Never talk of this,' Ballard said over the cubicle wall. Loud enough to be heard over both their expulsions.

'Of course, sir... of course.'
They were going to be later than planned.
Madder than expected.

***

Jimi called the boat back to pick him up. It couldn't get there soon enough.

He felt sick.

He thought: take him, dangle his hairy arse over a bridge, not the girls' though. Fuck me, what was he dealing with here — is there no honour left anywhere in the world.

'Let me off.'

'We're not at the landing spot yet.'

'Do it.'

He bunged the skipper fifty, jumped out to swim, then ran up the beach. Coughing his way down the streets, back to The Hell's Belles

When he got near and could see the front of the bar he cried.

It was the first drop spilt in anyone's company other than his own. And the first that wasn't left to dissolve away on Sand Point with his discarded bitter memories.

Tammy stood there. Smiling. Betty too... Two boxes lay at her feet, full of Jack Daniels.

'Thought you were running short, love,' she said.

He continued to cry.

They held him and all three stood strong. Jack appeared and stood in the doorway. Both girls nodded to each other, glanced knowing looks. Jack joined in. A moment shared, never to be forgotten. A bond. The untouchable knight had shown a chink in the armour — he was human after all.

'I've found us somewhere,' he said eventually when

they were back inside. 'We can live. Still do this,' he pointed to the bar. 'But, untouched by that...' he pointed to outside.

They got it. And were behind him two hundred and fifty per cent. He suggested they go ahead, set up camp, get themselves out of the firing line. Both were totally on board. They'd run the show from the island like grand commanders. Whilst setting up a pirate's haven...and the best sailors drinking den in a hundred years.

They were already dreaming of it. Could see it. Taste it.

Tammy could revamp the battery positions. Order in some lookout and gun replacement kit. Betty would handle CCTV, in charge of surveillance. Then, when Jimi was done they'd get the old, abandoned inn sorted. Injecting new lifeblood to the fishing lines that passed... But it would take too long. They needed help.

An hour later, the crews started to filter back in. Joking and laughing as they came. Except for the very serious stone-faced, Pitches and Hoes group. Or, Elite Security Squad as they were now known.

'Lads and lasses,' Jimi started when there were enough of them back in. 'There's an evolution, a development — a reworking of the plan.'

'What now?' Brian choked through his pint of Stella.

'Who fancies being a pirate?'

'Fuck yeah — ooh arghh!' was a unified response.

'I need volunteers. A lot of work to get our new place sorted. This here, The Belles...love of my life, is coming under the firing line — none of us is safe whilst this is our base,' he prioritised the girls and his son, Jack, in his head as he spoke. 'We need something more substantial. More solid,' and he laid out a map of the island they'd printed off on dozens of A4s and taped together... 'Gun batteries here. Need some work,' and he pointed. 'Old hospital here, needs a roof, generator, power, water...it'll be the barracks for you lot,' he jabbed again at the map on the floor. They leant in, craning to savour the details. Everyone's eyes were lit up, focussed, beyond excited. 'Landing jetty here, bay here. And... The inn here,' and he jabbed an exclamation. 'Our new centre. Home. The base for the commanders of the fleet,' and he pointed a thumb at the girls.

Then the girls took over, briefing and splitting them into teams. Half stayed behind with Jimi to delay the 'Cockney Rebels'. And the others were to go ahead to the island, order in materials, fix it up for the 'Builders Union'.

'Got a name for the place yet, Jimi, for the inn?' Mikey said.

'It'll always be The Hell's Belles... We make it, not the ground it's stood on.'

***

At dawn: like an invading Viking fleet, the first of them headed over on boats borrowed from some of Jimi's locals. Three boats filled with materials, raw woman power and eager workmen. Translucent peaks of crimson horses crested each wave and crashed down ahead of them, backlit by a blood-red sun.

The girls leant out from the head of their boats. They broke the waves as spray splashed up and over. Betty's silky black hair waved like a flag in the wind. Whilst Tammy's blonde locks wrestled around like a manic octopus, dripping salty waters on to those in the back. They smiled and lapped at it as if it was drops of christening breast milk from mother nature. All of them smiled towards a new, exciting world that awaited them on the shore of the island.

They landed but didn't run out.

They walked slowly up the stony shore. Feet sinking

into the pebbles. All savouring and absorbing the magic.

With each step the women took ownership. The Island felt meant to be. An heirloom and imagined destiny now made truth by Jimi's hopes for them all.

'Home,' Betty said looking up at the derelict inn up ahead. It was built into the steep hillside. And stretched down to the rocks of the shore below. A narrow doorway from the shore led up stone steps past the old cellars to the main room above.

They hovered outside, waiting for Tammy and Betty to break the seal even though there was no door, yet.

'The bar is the first to be fixed,' a lad's voice came from the back.

They paused.

The girls went in and the others waiting in-line on the steps. Like children waiting for parents' approval. One of the sparkies switched the torch of his multi-toll on and off, on and off, on and off.

As laughter and giggles began to echo down the old stone staircase; they knew it was time to go up.

***

They both waited for Imodium to set before advancing. Avoided the usual coffee or anything with vitamin c. Max would have drunk fresh concrete and stitched his own hole shut... he was so impatient to get going.

'Best hit the road, Captain Slack Arse,' Max said from the back.

Danny thought: he could have hit back with a retort. It wasn't his idea to stop for the rancid pig's flesh in a stale bap. Max was pissing outa his arse too a few moments ago — why had Danny become the sole trader in these shameful, dirty, unscheduled stop-off memories. Max would blame him that they were late too… He'd already threatened to take a finger if we weren't massively early. God, he needed to get out of this job as soon as possible. Not easy when your job is a driver, and you're driving you and your bitter employer headlong like a bullet into war.

'Righty o, sir,' he complied, reversed them out. He floored it as soon as they hit the dual carriageway. He had time to make up. It wouldn't be enough.

'Know much about this Jack lad, son?'

'Big sis went to school with him, in the year above,' Danny quivered. Hesitating to draw any connection between him and the dead man walking. Immediately he regretted mentioning his sister. He closed his eyes tight, the car was on cruise anyhow. Why did he have to go and do that? Because… Max Ballard could smell a lie, plant, or insincerity a mile off, usually. That's why.

What went wrong with Jack then? Why didn't he pick up on that deception?

Thing is when Jack talked to Ballard he was meant. Set on his purpose. He didn't know this Jimi man from Adam. And now… they're related.

Small fucked up inter-connected world.

If a tree falls in the Amazon maybe there is a hurricane in China.

And if you don't do your job in Weston-super-Mare… Give a little someone a seeing to. A fucking tidal wave of hurt is gonna wash down the M4 and blot out the landscape.

That black wall of water heading for town was Max Ballard.

***

Jimi and Jack played pool in the Captain's Cabin Bar, an old mock tutor boozer with views out to sea from every window. A beautiful musty smell clung to every low beam from two hundred years of damp fishermen's sweaters, ale, and pipe smoke.

Brian, Mikey, and Steve watched them play.

'When's the real storm coming, Jimi?' Mikey asked as Jimi went to break.

His cue hovered behind the white ball. Primed. Like a gun with a hairpin trigger. 'Well, those numpties that we dished out nasty hangovers to will soon perk up. Their boss will be breathing down their necks. And because Jack has come over to the dark side,' he winked in his direction, 'I reckon *he'll* be on his way. The main guy. And, unless he stops off to bunk up with the driver should be here any hour…if not already.'

'Who is he?'

'Ballard, Max-bastard-Ballard,' and he smashed the balls to oblivion. Pocketed three reds.

'Fuck me, isn't he some heavyweight champion badass of the world?' Brian yelped as the balls started to settle.

'Just another prick, got diverted away from hustling slots, bars, restaurants and skimming cash on some protection racket crap,' Jimi said 'and the thing is, we're doing a public service here. Whilst they're attempting to bust our bones they're leaving other people alone.'

'One way of looking at it, Jimi… But,' Stevie said, but was interrupted as the Elite Security Squad walked in, all looking at their iPhones.

'The eyes and ears have arrived — what's up, robocops?' Brian grunted then grabbed one of their phones. 'Nice, is this live?'

'Sure is.'

They cast it to the big screen behind the pool table,

ordered a round, closed the door...settled in.

On-screen the three brothers marched up and down the promenade. They had a gaggle of trench coat wearing gangster hanger ons with them. They stopped. About turned then walked the other way. A troop of gangster monkeys with nowhere specific to go.

'I don't get it. Why don't they just go hang out outside The Belles — looking to get the jump on us?'

'They're setting a tone. Want a presence to be felt. Have the people in fear, then they'll say we need to be ridden out of town. Shit man, haven't you seen the Westerns?' Jimi said through laughter.

Fourteen

A WHILE BACK, JIMI DID TIME. Not much. And not hard time. It wasn't Strangeways; he had plumbing and more than a few feet square to himself. The people and walls about him flexed and he'd settled right in. He looked the part. Like he'd been there from day one. His weathered stocky build with bald head got him respect in all the wrong places, and a bit of fear and reservation elsewhere. Even though inside his head, he was filled with confused sensitivities. Just like everyone else. Fighting his own battles. Feeling like he was always losing. Then, taking a breath and realising that was the real win, being able to.

He'd put his feet up; made some heavyweight new acquaintances both inside prison and for when he got out. He wasn't a criminal. Just had the sense to keep his mouth shut at the right time, for the wrong people… Depending on your moral compass. They didn't forget. From then on, they had his back. And when he got out, he was never without work. A roof here, a wall there. And they always paid. Often with a tip. And all-in cash. He didn't question it. Suited him just fine. He made some colourful new drinking buddies in The Cornubia pub too. It was a small Georgian boozer, with a loud parrot, a large beer garden too. And that's where he picked up most of his new business.

The Jags and Range Rovers would pull up. If not there already.

'Alright, Jimi?' How's it going? Got much on?' They'd say as soon as they clapped eyes on him.

'It's okay, can't complain. Bit quiet I suppose. Next week at least. Time to get a drink in. Pull a splinter or two out and let the calluses go down.'

'Met Barry here? Needs a new roof on his place,' they'd say with an arm around some nervous looking sap.

'Do I?' would come the shakey response from whoever they'd dragged along. It was a form of punishment and a show of strength to see the rest of the crew at the bar and smoking. Nodding on their every word. Even the parrot was on side.

They'd insist whoever they'd brought along paid out of the odds for Jimi's work. They'd take the deposit, and Jimi would get more than his fair share of the remaining payments.

'Yes, you fuckin' do, son. You're getting a new roof. Be lucky it's not the whole house,' they'd say. Sometimes a roof. Sometimes a garage. And they'd have to supply the materials.

The rest of the work Jimi got was direct for these local gangsters; on their houses, their families' ones too — he was good at what he did. And he'd kept his trap shut and had taken time for them.

Police had been watching them when they used to hang out at their previous favourite pub around the corner: The Shakespeare. Jimi was a regular there too. Although he hadn't been taken under the gang's wings by then. The police had watched, surveyed, and had Jimi down as one of them. Pinned his image to someone else, got confused, and were sure it was him driving that van on a bank job.

It wasn't.

His image didn't help with the jury. Telling them he sometimes cried himself to sleep wouldn't do shit. They took one look at his bald head, broad shoulders and troubled stare and decided: guilty. They only half looked at the police footage. Minds made up. He had got his hands dirty. But, in his usual line of work. Not how they thought.

***

'At what point, if any, are you gonna call your Bristol gangster pals?' Stevie said from his bar stool when they'd finished watching the CCTV stream.

'They've got their own shit going on. This isn't anything we can't handle, yet,' Jimi looked out to sea. Then turned slowly in the direction of the island and thought about the girls. He had it covered. 'Thing is. When we do that...there's no going back. You can't put the top back on that bottle. And we'll be aligned to all of them...we'll each be one of them. At this moment, we're just an annoyance that won't play along. A gang of pissed labourers with the town behind us.'

Mikey asked: 'What if they play heavy?'

'I've already been dangled out over the Avon Gorge and set alight...' Jimi spoke and Jack shrunk back in awkwardness. If he could have retracted his head into his shoulders like a retreating shy testicle, he would have.

'Sorry about that,' Jack winced.

'And… I'm sorry I left you to fend for yourself with your bat-shit crazy mother…'

A stillness took the room. With the uncertainty created by one person's words and in another's possible response. Until a reaction was made, the tone remained tense. A knife edge. They both gripped pool cues hard from the game earlier. Everyone else in the room could only wait — would there be blood spilt or blood bonded in what was said next. Jack could be tied tight to his mother. Most people are.

'Then I guess we're just about square,' Jack said and smiled.

Jimi started first. And then the others joined in —

the belly laughs came and the walls vibrated in unity.

The burns to Jimi's arms hurt like hell. But now something new inside made it all ok. Sedated him and his pain; made it bearable. Damn, it actually made the sensation something almost pleasant...to feel it and to know the burns were there. Eating away, reminding him who had put them deep into his skin. The marks to remain forever. Somehow, he felt Jack's heart beating from across the room. Each beat mirroring one of his own. Jack's blood was his blood. His life was his.

***

'Why'd we fucking drive, Danny? And not get the train instead,' Max said to the wall of stationary traffic to the front, side and rear of the car.

'Might as well have a dose, Max... Sorry, I mean, Mr Ballard... Who knows when this is gonna shift.'

'So... your sister. What'd she make of him?'

'Sorry, sir?' Danny really wished Max would just close his eyes and sleep. In fact, he wished he'd do that and not wake up — full stop. He thought: maybe he could pull over and make a run for it as Max counted sheep, guns, knife victims or whatever helped these gangland bosses relax. Or maybe, he could just quietly smother him in his sleep.

Max's eyes tightened. Suspicious at the thoughts he could see toiling away in Danny's head reflecting in the rear-view mirror.

Danny snapped to — worried Max could read his mind. He could see the devil in those piercing eyes as they glared back at him.

The cars moved forward a couple of lengths. Danny nudged them on.

'At school, what was he really like? This Jack lad...' Max insisted.

Danny thought hard before answering. To distance himself and family from the roaring issue in Max's head. He wouldn't mention that his sister had once a thing for Jack. That he'd walked in on them. His big sister had been riding Jack like a crazed jockey a half-length from the finishing line. They were both still in their school clothes. Her skirt up around her neck. Danny had nipped home to steal some fags from his sister room. And *they*...had nipped home for a quickie.

You couldn't unsee that kind of shit. He'd tried. And you couldn't override the nagging guilt and confusion having kept the door open a jar a moment too long when you realised what you were looking at. And enjoyed it. He'd played with himself and re-imagined it a few years since. Until he became sexually active and created his own dirty memories to recall. Now, again, the guilt mounted and confused him. Sometimes in his head, before climax, he was her. Sometimes, he was Jack. Every time he peaked with pleasure and a moment later he was disgusted; guilt-ridden.

'Son, wake up!' Max barked.

Danny was lost in a memory. He looked down to his bulging trousers and then to the rear-view mirror. He blushed in shame.

'Sir, yes.'

'Jack. At school!?'

'Bit aloof. A geek. A loser. Going nowhere. Think he was gay.'

'Thought you said your sister knew him.'

'Knew of him. Wasn't much to know. He wore black. Hung around with some other geeks. Shit at sports. Didn't get picked for anything...'

'That's quite a lot to know second hand. Sure they weren't fucking, your sister and Jack?'

How did that come full circle and back at him like that, Danny thought.

'You ever knock one out, whilst thinking of your sister?'

'I'd rather cut it off, sir,' seriously, Danny thought. The fucking Devil's a mind reader. He had to get out... Getaway. He wasn't going to survive this gangster war crap. He was just trying to make a few quid on the side moonlighting. Everyone was at it these days. The money wasn't enough behind the bar of The Black Sheep.

'If she's not a pig, you've done it. Or you're gay. Human nature is human nature. Can't fight it,' and he leant forward and looked at Danny crotch. Then slowly back up to his face.

Danny's hands shook on the wheel. He felt interrogated. Violated.

Max settled back into his chair and the traffic started to move a little, then it stopped again. This kid was an easy windup. One of the perks to being stuck with him on the long drive, he thought.

Max closed his eyes, smug. Content in the torment he'd imposed on another and slept.

A police motorbike passed their car. It dodged around the traffic like a manic bee through nettles to a sunflower, carving its way to the front of the queue; the accident, smash or pile up.

It slowed up ahead. Like the driver had forgotten something. What was more important than getting to the incident? The driver made a call on the radio and looked back at Max and Danny's car.

'Sir, better wake up...' Danny hesitantly let out. 'Sir, please... Wake up!'

'What the fuck now, son?'

'Up there. Trouble.'

'Fucking busies. Haven't they got enough to be getting on with — moving this traffic?' as Max spoke the bike's rider stared at them, mouthing more on their radio.

Then, like a heat-seeker catching the scent of a hotter engine, they slowly turned the bike around and homed in on a new target: them.

'Tell PC whoever-the-fuck I'm passed out, ill or something. That we were headed out for a drive… To clear our heads or something. And wake me up when they've gone,' Max closed his eyes. Crossing his arms in defence of what was to come.

Danny shook. He *really* wasn't cut out for this shit.

'Help,' he whispered under his breath.

'What you say, son? Grow a fucking pair,' came Max's stone-cold words from the back.

The motorbike neared and gave a flash of its lights and siren for effect. A warning.

'Tap tap tap,' came the knuckles on the driver side.

Danny took a shaky hand from the steering wheel and pressed the button to open his window. And with it pushing his anxiety levels to near breaking point. He could hear his heart beating in his ears. And the sweat to his palms and finger that still pulled the button back even though the window was now fully down.

'Now then, boys,' the WPC said, lifting her visor.

Danny saw that she was hot. A little like his sister. This didn't help.

'Where're you off to with, *him*? This car is marked. Take it out of London, anywhere, and you'll have people breathing down your necks. You can just about move it around the block or to Aldi and that's about it…at least without raising the alarm bells,' she said to Danny but directed it at Max. She knew he was listening and threw him a glance.

'He's passed out ill. Had the shits earlier. A bit dehydrated,' too much information, he thought. The words just came out though. He couldn't help it. Couldn't lie. He had the same problem at school. It was an authority thing. A uniform thing. And definitely a talking to girls thing. His legs shook now too. Was he going to wet himself — who knows, he thought, just get through this...

One of Max's eyes opened in the back. The one out of sight. It reddened, bloodshot and full of fury. The piece in his jacket felt heavy. The temptation to take out the copper and this waste of space driver were boiling him up inside. Both were specks of dust. Wasting his time. His temples pounded. He had somewhere to be.

'What's the hold-up, miss?' Max said, calm, polite... zen-like, from the back. Eyes fixed shut again.

'You and your crew are under surveillance, Max. How you've got this far I dunno,' she said.

'We haven't got very far at all... Have we?' Max said.

'Take the next roundabout. This will all get moving in an hour or so. Just moving a jack-knifed lorry and a family of four that met it head-on. Now, get back to the city.'

'Sorry to hear that. Real sorry,' Max muttered.

'We're just out... clearing our heads,' Danny said.

'Yes, a lot on our minds. It's all got a bit much in the big smoke. Getting a bit...'

'Claustrophobic,' she finished Max's sentence for him.

'Yes, thank you, officer,' Max said, meekly. As if talking to a priest.

Up ahead the traffic shifted and moved on. They were left alone to their roadside interrogation.

'You could have changed the number plates, Max. Not exactly discrete are they? Her eyes slowly swapped back and forth between Max and Danny.

'I guess,' he said.

'That's your pride there, Max. Arrogance. A misplaced sense of your place in the world,' she goaded him. Now he was the one being wound up. So tight... he was so close to taking the safety off the holstered gun in his jacket...

One more stab of her tongue and he wasn't sure he could hold it any longer. Pop-pop. That's all it would take. Bundle her in the boot then get back on with the journey.

'Sandra?' Danny asked, looking at her badge.

She fixed her eyes on him. Her eyes stopping their dance between them.

'Yes...do I know you?'

'You went to school with my sister didn't you?' he said.

She blushed... A discarded memory made its way to the front: a sleep-over, someone's brother coming out of the shower, a dropped towel, and her bending to pick it up for him. A lingered moment too long in front that turned into something more playful. Kissing it. Grabbing those cheeks to pull him in harder...

This wasn't him. Couldn't be.

'Never met you or your sister,' she said regaining some composure. Now all three held a nervous rattled awkwardness, uncertain where to go to next.

Danny was confused by her blushing and sudden shift in confidence. He'd never seen her before. He just thought an idle shift of focus away from the car and into her head might do them all some good. It was debatable whether the shift had worked. The air was now filled with an awkward stalemate of unsaid vulnerability in the front, and the unexploded bomb in the back: Max.

'Will do, miss,' Danny said, 'we'll get back asap.'

Her radio blurted. Breaking the tension. Panicked voices, shouts, feedback... codes... numbers... more words then shouts.

She was off. Like a rocket. And for now, they were free to go.

Fifteen

PAT LYNCH LIKED JIMI. Jimi had taken a year or two inside rather than rat one of Pat's top drivers out. And whilst Jimi was doing that time, the same driver had made some serious money for Pat. Fuck...he actually loved Jimi.

They had shared a few drinks in The Cornubia. Chatted through life's ups and downs. When they could get a word in over the fucking parrot.

Pat had started setting Jimi up with work — to pay him back for keeping his mouth shut. He made sure the debt was paid over him taking the time for them.

It could have gone on happily like that forever.

Pat was gutted when Jimi mentioned he was going to move out. Jimi had said he wanted to wind down, play his guitar. Get the hard skin on his fingertips from the strings rather than the palms of his hands from the bricks, wood, and cement.

Fair dues, Pat told him. He wasn't a criminal. He deserved the easy run down to death if he wanted it. Rather than the sudden exclamation mark and block on the line that usually came in Pat's line of work.

'So long, Jimi. And if you ever need anything... you've got our number,' Pat said over their last drink together.

Pat gave Jimi a little money now and again. A bit of whatever that driver made from each of his jobs from then on. No questions asked. Jimi tried to refuse. Said what he did was some sort of street respect thing. Honour amongst thieves… Pat told him to drink up and take it.

And so every now and again, usually once a month,

Jimi got a small injection of funds. At first, it kept him up at night wondering who had lost out so he was gaining. He knew Pat and his lads specialised in corporate and bank fuck overs so it didn't last long. Soon he was sleeping like a baby with a new teether every month.

***

'Max Ballard is heading down the M4. Trying to anyhow. He's got beef with Jimi,' one of them said to Pat in The Cornubia.

'Max Ballard. Bad bastard,' the parrot squawked.

'Bad bastard indeed, Poly,' Pat said. 'What does a big-time London tosser like that want with our Jimi?' and he picked up his phone from the bar. Began to dial. Each number pressed opened a floodgate of pressure getting closer between them and the London mob.

They had an arrangement. Firmly defined and agreed turfs. There was no need to tread on anyone's feet. Max looked down on the West Country like it was small pickings and full of cider chugging simpletons. Pat let him have his generalised dig. Told him it was the Graveyard of Content. And unless he wanted to join, to stay out.

'Pat. Long time,' Max said from the other end of the line. 'What can I do for you? Bad reception, driving... So, make it interesting or you might get cut off.'

'What's all this I hear about you having beef with our Jimi?'

'Your Jimi is it? What's he to you, Pat? Interesting. Very fucking interesting. I thought he was just a white van driving moron who'd learned a few power chords... A retired meat-head builder who stood in the way of us a bit too long.'

'In the way of what, Max? Weston's not your patch.

Fuck, it's not even mine. It's the Wild West out there. Looks after itself...'

'That so...?' Max interrupted. 'Well, how's about I just ride in and start creating a little order to the place? Fancy me a donkey ride anyhow. Might as well be there.'

'Seriously, Max. Jimi's a good lad. Leave it alone. Isn't Brighton more your thing?'

'Sometimes, it depends on which way the wind's blowing. And my persuasion.'

'Come on, Max. You don't want this.'

'Don't tell me what I do and don't want. It's gone too far, Pat... We're down to principles now. Sometimes, and you know it yourself, Pat, dogs need a kicking every now and again. To feel the masters boot in. To be reminded who's the alpha. And this one... well, he's had a kicking...and burning. Still hasn't rolled over. So, I'm gonna take care of it, personally,' Max omitted any detail to do with Jack: his new failed recruit. The real reason for the trip. Unless Pat mentioned him, he didn't see any benefit in spilling his cards out on the table like that.

'Max... you don't want to do this. I thought you were laying low whilst all that London Bridge crap blew over?'

'Nothing to do with us, Pat. Maybe that was you?'

'You know fine well... We stay out of your shit, Max. Unless invited. How's about you stay out of ours?'

'Said it yourself, Pat: Weston's free game. Out of your jurisdiction...' he paused... 'Pat.'

'Yes, Max.'

'There's a new sheriff comin' to town...'

CLICK: Max hung up.

'This isn't going to end well,' Pat said to the room. They'd all been hanging on his every word. His mobile hit the bar top with a thud and another round appeared: Thatchers Gold with a rum chaser.

'End well, it isn't,' the parrot squawked.

'Nope, Poly. It isn't,' Pat admitted.

'Fuck. Ballard. Twat,' Poly said.

'Aye,' Pat nodded and drank it down to a half-pint down in one go. Then he went outside for a smoke and to discuss the next moves with his crew.

One of three girls, the brains of the outfit, said: 'He can't be planning on playing too rough. It'd be career suicide with all the heat around them at the moment. Those crazy-assed brothers fucked up that London Bridge job; sprayed body parts all of the river-Bank and the Tate car park. Surely the police have them wound-up pretty tight. Surprised they let them out of London at all... Any of 'em.'

Pat told them they'd likely be aiming to play soft, by their standards. Have a little fun. Bit of roughing people up. Old-school style. Like Mad-Friday on a long weekend in The Hen and Chicken.

They knew what he meant. The Hen and Chicken was a Bristol City supporters pub. It could get a bit rough, spilling out onto the streets. The poor bar staff would find themselves breaking up family feuds, friends, enemies, a secret Rovers supporter that had sneaked in and got found out. It was very old-school, fists. No knives. No guns. The losers were carted away ashamed. The winners got respect and sometimes put in the back of a police van to cool off. An ambulance was rarely needed. Unless some out-of-towners mistook their place and tried to get involved.

'Problem is...' Jimi went on, 'this Max Ballard character... Well, he's got a reputation to uphold. If they'd just left it, early days, it could have died down. But now Ballard's hackles are up and he's got an exposed jugular in his sights. He won't back down. Not ever. He's like a raging pit bull.'

'What'll we do then, Pat?' one of the lads in the group

asked and lit Pat's rolly.

'Delay Max... And wait for the call. Jimi's a big boy. If he was feeling the pinch, scared, or in need, he'd have called.'

'Really?'

'No... He's one principled hard stubborn bastard too. How'd you think we've got so close and love him so much. Fuck, this is going to be messy,' Pat said. His expression looked grave, then came the upturn of a lip with a twinkle of an eye, and he laughed... 'I can't fucking wait.'

Inside, the parrot rocked backwards and forwards as age-old dust settled. It had been blown from the curtains for the first time in fifty years, maybe more. A small feather dropped from the bird as it took a shit, making a noise on the cage like a bell.

'Last orders,' the parrot squawked, 'Time's up!'

'Shut it, Poly,' Pat said. 'Get another round in. We've got some thinking to do.'

***

Max had been daydreaming, playing with the freshly forming scars to his hands from the broken glass, when the call came. He saw Pat's name on the screen and told Danny to put it on speakerphone. He knew he'd worried them, stoked a little fire some and settled back to see if took hold. It was a broken line, a shit reception, but Max got the gist: Pat wanted Max not to go to Weston. Jimi meant something. As far as he was concerned the whole West Country was out of bounds. As Pat talked Max thought: I've left them sleepy bastards to have it easy over there for far too long. They need to pay their way. Join the fold or move aside.

Max got bored of listening to Pat. He'd sounded like a stoned pirate and Max didn't have the patience. He hung up and the speakers hissed and clicked dead. He sat back for a think: this is going to be even more fun. What's with these South West country bumpkins.

'Why don't they just stick to hay baling and Cider with Rosie?' Max said.

'I dunno, Max… What's that all about?'

'You don't know much, Danny-son. Don't worry yourself.'

Max breathed out.

Danny held his in.

The traffic stopped, again. Then, Max spoke. Not because he cared what Danny thought, or because he valued his opinion. 'These days… Our trade is down to a few old hangers-on. It's all digital now. No one really gets their hands dirty anymore.'

'Yes, Max.'

'Shut up, Danny.'

'Okay, Max.'

'The thing is it's easier to message a million saps and demand they deposit some PayPal funds. Or you'll release a video of them jerking off to the site you bought their email address from. There's no honour in that. Fuck, might as well set up a sweatshop call centre and ring a hundred pensioners a day telling them to buy a new footstool. Handmade in the U.K. via Vietnam. No, times have well and truly changed son. Me, Pat, The Cricketers, last of a dying breed son. Robbing from the rich corporates, or the other less worthy gangs, and leaving the innocents alone. Makes me sick when you think of what's going on now. Phishing, what the fuck is that bollox. Spamming, who gives a crap. Look someone straight in the eyes, tell them they're a cunt and why you're taking what they've got — why you're more worthy than they are. That's where all this is wrong. No honour,' Max said, took another breath and sighed. Genuinely ratted. He didn't like change.

As his mind came to rest, he realised he'd gone totally off-piste in this whole escapade. This wasn't about Jimi, Jack or even Pat. This was a last go at being a known quantity in the underworld. The lines had got blurred, confused. A fat anonymous man eating a family bag of Monster Munch in his pants, on a laptop in a darkened room was a success on paper in this game now.

Max wanted a last go at it, the old-fashioned way: face to face action. A holiday at the seaside with some good old-fashioned face-offs, dressing downs and buried out at seas — if it came to that.

'We might have to take another route. The police will realise we haven't double-backed at some point. And anyhow, this traffic sucks — we're not getting anywhere fast,' Danny said.

'If you know a better way to get West. Other than this big, massive road, pointing West. Take it. Otherwise, we're just gonna have to plod on and get there when we get there. Besides, where else do you have to be that's more interesting than here, with me, going there?'

'Sisters birthday tomorrow, sir. Thought we'd have got to Weston by now and I'd be on my way back.'

'Slag,' Max barked.

Danny's nerves hadn't calmed since earlier. When he'd thought his ears were going to explode. His worries had now gestated, spread throughout his body. His veins carried the burden, his blood flowing with the lead weight of his trapped predicament. It wasn't his sister's birthday. He was just looking for an out. Any out. Whilst his mouth said polite excuses not to be there, his brain was doing overtime. Still thinking of an escape. Maybe he could poison Max? Anything, he just needed out. It was life or death now. He knew it now. This Max character was a fucking monster and they'd just past Swindon; had another 60 odd miles to go. And, at this rate that could be hours...days even.

Danny took stock. What did he have? He thought: there's Max's gun. If I could get it from him when he next sleeps. Thing is, it'd be like sticking your head in a crocodile's mouth to extract a tooth to trying and stab it with. No, not a good idea. Could Danny even figure out how to fire the thing? He'd likely be pissing around with the safety as Max's senses came too. And Max snatched it back and caved his face in with the butt of it. Max wouldn't even waste a bullet on him right now. He could hear it in his voice.

Or... the lighter fluid in the glove box for Max's Zippo. Yes, he could spray it everywhere. Light the demon up and run for the fields.

He could see it now: The flaming car behind him. Max's rage as his gun fired off in all directions. As Ballard seared alive engulfed by flames in the back seat. Locked in, unable to release the doors. And Danny would run. Legs burning with effort, the release; finally free of him. Smiling, looking ahead. Running so hard through the high cornfield towards the nearest house. He'd stumble picking himself up, but he'd get there — away. An old dear would say: Oh you poor thing come in. She'd make a pot of tea. He'd take a biscuit...a slice of cake. Collapse into an armchair to tell her all about it. And she'd smile. And a little spaniel would run into lap at his weary hands. Oh dear, yes. Heavens to Betsy, she'd say.

Then, she'd grin... Her eyes would blacken over. Blood would pool and drip from her eyes, as a violent rage took over her mouth. And those teeth, sharp, snapping... Chipping away as she angrily chomped. The cakes would fly, covered in blood as the tea boiled over in all the cups and pot. The cup he held would rattle in its saucer. She was Max. Her dog that bit at his ankles was Max too. The bird in a cage in the corner of the room was Max. Squawking: wake up. Wake up. Wake up.

The car swerved, hitting a traffic cone. Vibrations from the layby studs rattled the shell of the Merc.

'WAKE UP!' Max shouted.

Danny had been going into a mental loop for some time. Like a crashed computer well overdue a service update. Forgetting he'd switched from cruise control, he'd been half asleep at the wheel. Mentally exhausted and scheming in the darkest recesses of his brain. And even there, where his subconscious and conscious wrestled over his core self, Max was there. Waiting to attack, like a hungry shark at an injured seal pup.

'Wake the fuck… UP!'

And then he was back in the cage on wheels. With a real-life monster: Max.

Sixteen

JIMI SWITCHED THE CCTV STREAM back onto the pub's big screen. On it, the brothers and their posey made their way up the high street. The local shell suits, single mums, drunks, wasters, and pissheads didn't care. The out-of-towners could have been dressed in pink lycra with boas around their necks and no one would blink an eye. Instead, everyone's eyes looked down into the pavement, for solace in a penny dropped, a dress shoplifted or a strangers phone left unguarded.

Everyone had a personal axe to grind. The town was hurting long before the Cricketers came to town. The people had nothing left to take; their lives a daily torment with no way out but for a drink or wrap of something to take the edge off.

An old lady pushed her tartan shopping cart through a bunch of teenage boys. Like a wounded whale through a school of hungry young tiger sharks. They leered, weighing her up. Her cart was as empty as their pockets and they left her alone. She nodded, giving a strained smile on the way through. They tried a smile. And a mutual unsaid respect from either end of the strained age-poverty-chain in town was exchanged.

The brothers homed in on the old lady. Eyeing her from across the street,

Jimi and the pub sat up, focusing on the TV.

The three brothers left their clan on one side of the street and walked over to intercept the old dear. They bent down, whispered something. She stood still, haunched. An age of pain, struggling and a dead husband behind her — she wasn't easily moved these days.

'Is that… Rose?' Jimi said sitting up. Knowing damn well no one in the room knew anyone from the town but him and the girls. 'They're brave if they're trying to put the willies up that. Fuck me. There's an age-old Welsh dragon in there waiting to breathe fire at them.'

Sure enough, the old lady slowly raised her head. Even over the flickering CCTV footage, her blackened over eyes came across like coals in snow. The walking dead already, all she wanted was to cash her Giro cheque, get pissed up on sherry in The Criterion boozer, then pass out in front of *Columbo*. And if she made it as far as *Murder She Wrote* it was a good day.

Onscreen the brothers were clearly confused. What the hell was this?

Jimi smirked and the rest of the room mirrored him.

'Looks like she's got back-up,' Jack said.

They watched onscreen as the teenage boys looked over at the old lady and strolled over to encircle the brothers. The gangster troop saw this and walked over to form a bitterly tense series of concentric circles. The old woman was at the epicentre, with the brothers, then shell-suited teens and the gangland trench coats to the outskirts. A view from the top would have made a best-selling *Ikea* or *Habitat* poster. Over the CCTV it was a crime noir farse: like Laurel was about to turn, holding a ladder on his shoulders. And Hardy was about to get it face-on.

The old lady leant forward to the nearest brother. Whispered something.

Jimi and the pub could only guess what… It looked like it had an emphasised F, K and C in it.

She cracked the brother in the shin with her shoe. They could feel it half a mile away in the pub as they sat, gripped. All parts of the ring of baffled men and teens surrounding her jumped outwards.

The old lady picked up her trolley handle from the floor and strolled forwards. Leaving the teenagers, brothers and gang too confused shrugging and angry hand waving. They soon gave up and dispersed as the brothers attempted to regain order in the ranks.

'Shall we just go home? Not sure you need us here Jimi,' Stevie said to Jimi.

'I could have warned them. Columbo starts in an hour. She's got a cheque to cash and probably got a thirst on.'

***

At sundown, Jimi and Jack left the crews to it; told them to go have some fun. To stir things up — but stay safe.

'There's a place I want to show you,' Jimi said to Jack when they were alone. 'Somewhere I've been doing a lot of thinking. And my thoughts have been getting washed, listened to...'

'You're not gonna dangle me over the Severn Bridge, are you? I told you... I'm sorry.'

'Not tonight.'

Jack felt the grave weight and sorrow to Jimi's words. Jimi's eyes looked embarrassed and uncertain. Like Jack might refuse. Or was it a fear of Jack's response when they got there?

Jimi didn't want to leave Jack when he was a child. He was a loyal 'till death do us...' kind of man. He had to leave Jack's mother. It got that bad: like death.

One time Jimi was sounding off, telling some poor guy soon to have earache in the Black Sheep in Oval, all about it... Her temper, the confusion. Not being able to do right by wrong. The guy laughed and told him there's always going to be worse things than being on your own.

He didn't get it at the time. Then he had upped and left Jack and his mother. The jeans he was wearing and a black holdall were all he had.

Then, he got it.

Sand Point took ten minutes. Jack's van was fast, but he drove it slow by his standards. The winding single-lane coastal paths did nothing for his nerves and head. And most of all, he wasn't sure what was going on in Jimi's mind. They'd hardly said a word. Other than Jimi's: straight on, straight on, keep left, straight on...

Eventually, Jimi told him: 'There, the car park on the right by those bushes.'

Jack had spent too long in the city. It looked beautiful.

A grassy rocky outcrop rose up above them to the left. Having driven alongside the quietest stretch of sand, night or day, Jack had ever seen. Provided Jimi didn't throw him off the tip of The Point he wanted to come back.

The shrubs, trees and foliage curved up and around the steep narrow path they were on, casting spider-web-looking shadows from a full moon's glow.

'Watch out for dog shit,' Jimi said, taking the edge off an otherwise tranquil atmosphere.

The canopy opened up. A sky full of stars lay on top of the grass and the stony crest up ahead. Gulls called as other sea birds chattered in the background. The sea crashed its waves against the rocks below as the wind blew around both their bodies, sweeping away the day's worries.

'What a place.'

'It is that, son.'

They walked up further along towards The Point and the grass grew sparse as the rocks became more common. Then there was nowhere left to go. They were at the tip of the peninsular. High up over the waves. Looking out over to the Bristol Channel at the lights of South Wales.

Jimi sat on a hard pitted rock and Jack sat alongside.

'They know about this place. Fucked my tyres up last time I was here.'

'Are we safe then?' Jack asked.

'I reckon we could take them. Me and you. We'd hear them coming. Be able to take them down. Guerrilla warfare style. One at a time. Working the shadows and pouncing. '

'Nice.'

'Besides, I had to show you this place.'

'Dad,' Jack said and could see Jimi's nearest eye was welling up, again, on his use of the D-word. This time he knew it. He'd weekend a beast. Softened the hard man. He should never have come on this job. What were the chances of meeting him? And now he has… The irony. Meeting your father whilst on a job to rough him up, getting close to him, and then that's the thing that weakens him… As the gangsters you work for come to wreak revenge. Leaving him defenceless. 'You up to this?' he said and put a hand on his father's shoulder.

'Don't worry, son. It takes a real man to cry. I used to do it here in secret. All my purging, alone. Now you're here too. To hear me out. When we walk down from here. The place where I did all my thinking. We'll be knights. Bound forever,' and then he told him: everything. Why he'd left his mother. How he'd spend hours sitting up there on The Point and thought about him… Imagining Jack with a wholesome real-life, an education, city desk job. How Jimi'd thought he'd pollute it if he ever showed face. So, he just stayed away. For Jack's own good. It was a bitter twisted love and loss born out of self-loathing, Not wanting to have Jack near him. But also for fear of his mother.

'I had all that, dad. The education, desk job and the rest. It must be in the blood though. I came round to following your path anyway. It's destiny, dad.'

'I was never a gangster, son… Despite what people say or think. Kept my hands clean… kind of. Suppose it's what they call, ironic. Given what I really do or did: building work. Besides, I think that's more my brother you have in mind, John. The gangland black-star you're thinking about.'

'I've got an uncle?'

'That and then some...'

'Is he in deep — with this sort of thing?'

'Last I heard he was a writer, with dark tendencies. And some questionable connections in Manchester, Moss Side and Longsight. The type you don't wanna play with. In fact, I don't think the South Bank Cricketer lot would be too happy to play ball with 'em either.'

'So why isn't he here, taking care of it, and us on that island?'

'If you think I ain't touched a civil base with you and your mother in an overdue while, it's well overdue with him…no hope. He's literally won wars single-handed, at home and away. He could write a book or two on it… In fact...'

'You're taking the piss.'

'No, and we don't want to end up in one of those books son. There are no good guys versus bad guys in them. Just bad up against worse. And no one wins.'

The wind got colder. The birds grew silent. Adding an icy exclamation to Jimi's words.

'You could have been so good at it, dad...' Jack said after a moment's grace.

'I'm much worse than them, Jack. I'm a retired builder with a very loud Gibson SG,' Jimi said and nature restated. The birds called and the waves crashed on. The wind blew a sea spray into their faces — they felt alive.

They sat awhile until the stone ached their arses as

they laughed at the moon. Then, they walked back down the slope together. Through the bushes, shadows, and trees. Like the point had absorbed them in as separate and was birthing them back out, now together. A two-man army. As strong as the limestone they'd sat on.

'What happened with mother?' Jack asked on the drive back. Already feeling he knew the answer.

The silence said it all.

***

What happened between Jimi and Jack's mother?:

Martha would have taken a bullet for Jimi. Not today, she thought.

No, not today.

His early starts and mid-afternoon finishes got to be too much. She'd been up all night for months, feeding, changing nappies. All-day as well. Her body was a shell and her mind had gone to mush. The only thing going in his favour was that she couldn't think straight and her rationale was long since compromised.

She did the hard relentless slog every day, whilst fixing meals out of the thin air and the fuck all he brought home from work most days. He told her there was a long-term plan; to build a crew. That didn't count for shit without sleep and a baby to feed.

Meanwhile, he'd be clocking off from whatever site he was working on and be in the pub with his boys by 3.30 pm. An average builder's afternoon in the city. Most of them were stone stop — she guessed at least she was lucky he wasn't too.

Sleep-deprived, hungry, and breastfeeding was a bad combination for marital bliss.

Jimi said he was working hard. That the social after

work was part of it. Networking, he said, to find the best crews for future work. Crews he could rely on.

'Bollocks', she'd said before he left that morning. And then asked him when was the last time he changed a nappy, rocked Jack to sleep, rubbed her aching back or just put the fucking bins out. Oh, and they were out of milk... Ironic given she was aching and sore from feeding the boy. She yelled at him for the last time as he left for work. Her own milk dripped from red chaffed and cracking nipples. Staining a paper-thin stretched and torn top she wore; no longer affording time to her own appearance.

No, not today, she thought.

Today was the last day he played father when it suited. She'd be better off alone.

And what about the boy? He'd never know.

She'd already decided before Jimi had finished half-drunkenly fumbling with his key to get back in that evening. She wasn't going to let him in her, the flat or their lives again.

Jimi dropped the flowers and kids-sized A-Team shirt he'd picked up at lunch. The look in her eyes curdled the milk in his bag he'd bought too...

In his line of work, he had believed he could fix anything.

Not today.

He realised then that was when something broke, the pieces weren't going to fit back together again. Like a broken plastic plate, melting in a fireplace.

Seventeen

BETTY AND TAMMY SAT on the shore in front of the old inn. They loved the island; a new home. But they needed Jimi to make it rock. The cool water lapped at their bare feet as the waves sound massaged their inner calm, for now. Something was waiting to come to the surface. A dark presence, outcome, a cloud of change against them threatening change.

They felt it in the distance, getting closer: Ballard.

'We should record the sounds of these waves. Sell it to sleep-deprived parents,' Betty said.

'White noise… Could sell a few of Jimi's riffs too. Brown noise for Guantanamo Bay,' Tammy laughed and Betty smiled… It was a nervous distraction from an imminent threat.

They'd slept together spooning in sleeping bags zipped together into a triple. The hole where Jimi once lay between them closed tight shut beneath arms and legs. Comforted by the feel of each other's skin, they knew they'd closed down space between them where another person could fit. It was always his.

They missed him, more than words.

The inn was home and a base. The roof was now few tiles short of being complete and they'd accepted its embrace, with a hug by the fire and idle chat after a hard day's graft with the crews. The wooden beams and thick stone walls oozed a history of those that had sweated, bled, and toiled over the seas and island before them. It celebrated a return of life within its walls.

They lay back together, eyes gazing up from the stone floor. Reflecting stars. Lost in the vastness of space before the morning brought them back to earth.

Then it came: the morning.

The crews swapped shifts with those onshore. The Elite Security Squad arrived to set up a perimeter, security, and tripwires. Cheap laptops were set up at the inn, old hospital, and gun batteries. With power, they could now charge their phones and pull a stream to hand too.

They were all set.

Jimi rang: 'How's that inn...our new Belles coming along?'

'There's something missing, Jimi — It's missing you.'

'Miss you too, Tammy,' Jimi sounded nervous.

'What is it, pet?'

'This bad bastard, Ballard... He should have got here by now.'

'You sound scared, Jimi,' as she said it, she realised, she hadn't seen or heard him scared of anything much before. As her painted chipped nail scraped at hundred years of tar and grease from the thick wooden bar, she knew this, Ballard was a bad wind blowing their way. 'How was last night?'

'Me, the boys and girls might have a few bumps and bruises when you see us next,' Jimi touched his blackening eye and bruised nose. No breaks. 'It was like a saloon fight everywhere we went. No showdown or duels at dawn though... Not yet. They threatened us with Max Ballard. Said he was due there any second. You could see it in their eyes. They're more scared of him than we are. He must be something... Bad fucking work.'

'How about you put in that call Pat to the Bristol mob. Get yourself over here and leave them all to fight it out?'

'It's me and Jack he's after. Wants revenge. For a loss of face. I'm not sure letting the Brothers' runt play the stage is gonna cut it anymore… Ballard wants Jack's soul and my body. Drowned and sunk.'

***

Ballard was raging down the phone.

The brothers had nowhere to hide: 'I'm running out of fucking bottles to piss in. I've been my pecker out the window to piss on truckers and family hatchbacks. What's it with this sodding road? Been travelling overnight now… Still stuck. Might as well have run there.'

'Sorry, Max,' The Narrator said.

'Sorry, Max,' came The Echo in the background.

'You gooney arsed fuckers need to get it together. Pub brawls aren't enough. Get this shit wrapped up before I get there. I want to be revelling in Jimi and Jack's pain, suffering and downfall when I arrive — sort it!'

'Yes, Max.'

***

The night before, Jimi and the crews onshore had a little drink in each of Weston's holes. They'd decided to make it fancy dress. So, to blend in a little. By standing out. Stag-do style, in a town full of them.

The theme was fur. By the end, it was sweat, blood and beer. With scorched, singed undertones of fake hair.

Mikey, Brian, and Stevie looked like the three Stooges in old ladies drag. Jimi, with his fur hat, coat, and trouser combo, was more like a rough Chewbacca or a bear. Snazaroo face paint and inflatable golf clubs completed all their looks. A mass of furry builders out on a pub crawl golf round. Nothing unusual here.

***

Russel, or Russ, was ex-RAF. And Lou, was Royal Navy. Lou's ship had taken a battering during WWII and he'd lost close friends and his ears still rang from shell shock. He'd spent every day since he'd reached shore back when he was still in his teens, smiling and making jokes. He found and made every reason to be happy. To be alive. He figured he owed it to those who hadn't made it.

His japes and constant tomfoolery grated on his wife, who pretended to be tired of it, but loved him more than life. His best friend Russell and she feigned most of the irritation at him. Lou's constant shifts from one joke and superficial quip to another kept Russ from disappearing up his own more serious arse. And reminded Lou's wife there was another way: glass half full. When often, she didn't even see the glass at all.

Ross and Lou made a great double act, and they knew it. Lou the joker. Russ very much the straight man.

Russ had been waiting in the Weston Sports Bar for twenty-five long minutes. His feet had stuck to the thick busy patterned carpet and his eyes stung from the two screens in every direction. They showed horses, rugby, football, the dogs, boxing...it exhausted him to be there, and if Lou didn't show soon, he was going to leave.

Russ was never late, always early. Lou would drift in when he was ready as usual, and with a big smile on his face. Russ was too proud for these places. And Lou loved arranging to meet him in bars just like it, to wind him up.

'Why here Lou? You know I hate these new places. They're pits. Full of youths downin' Jager-bombs. Getting in the way of the screen. Shouting over us trying to talk,' Russ said before Lou sat down. His tall frame and flat cap cast a shadow over the empty small table that Russ glared up from.

'Just to see you squirm, Russ, old chap. Just to see *you*... squirm.'

'How's Sheila?'

'Told her I'd gone fishing with Captain Rod up-his-ass.'

'Charming.'

'How's your's indoors?'

'I shifted her from the mantlepiece to the conservatory the other day. To get a bit of sun,' and there was a crack in the stern facade, a glint in Russ's eyes. His wife was cremated years ago and he loved that Lou still asked how she was… They were all close when she was alive. 'The bar's over there. Just past the wall of chavs,' Russ said. 'Mind you don't get your pockets picked!'

'Not a problem,' Lou smiled and picked up Russ's wallet from the table. 'It's on you,' and he walked off with a fervent spring in his step.

The wait seemed even longer to Russ this time. Even though he could see Lou. Maybe it's because he knew Lou's idle flirting with the young barmaid was immeasurable. He could be a minute, he could be a half-hour.

'Pint of Guinness for me,' Lou said on his return, three minutes later. 'And... a Guinness and blackcurrant for the lady,' and he put Russ's down with a purple swirl spoiling an otherwise perfect pour.

'Lou, you old sod. You're getting a Taboo next.'

'Russ, you don't have the brass to order anything other than an ale up there.'

'I'll do it, Lou, I'll damn well do it...'

'I'll have a Babysham then, see how you get on asking for that.'

'What the...?' Russ's words were caught short as his head span round to see what the cat dragged in. As he was reeling from the taste of Lou's prank, six or seven trench coat-wearing shadows walked in. Sucking what little light there was from the room and obscuring most of the views to screens. 'What they come as, a posse or something?'

'Just another stag do. Sometimes those things are *crazy*. Other times, well, how can I put it. They're just a bit more straight-laced. Just plain weird looking.'

'That's what that is, is it? You thought they'd be smiling some.'

'Not everyone was as lucky as us, Russ lad. It might be a forced affair. A shotgun wedding. Times up for someone,' and Lou put a comedy gun finger to his head and pulled the trigger.

They were laughing it off as the door blew open again. The empty packets of Scampi Fries and Pork Scratchings that lay victim to their thirst danced in the wind, as the door was clamped open by a giant furry arm. Then one, two three, four...they lost count, what looked like bears, walked in. Slowly, playful and gave Russ and Lou a tickle under the chin on the way past.

'Next pub,' Russ said. Cold, a matter of fact, looking like a proud sergeant major too stiff to look at a stripper walking past.

'No way,' we have to see how this plays out.

Before long it was a mass of trench coats and furry assed bears in there, sweating. Russ and Lou were transfixed, gripped and nothing had happened much yet. They could feel it though. Like when a hen party meets a stag do. It's an unstoppable force against an immovable object. Drunk versus drunker.

Lou loved it and Russ studied it.

'You finished them damn journals you been writing up?' Lou said.

'They're always flowing, every night. Just lacking the final bit. Something interesting to close them down for a

while. Some new material and experience. Maybe this us it,'
and Russ waved at the mass of fur and trench coats at the
bar.

'Get them in, Russ.'

'You wanna short, Scotch this time?'

'I do, Russy, Mc Russ-Russ,' Lou said in a fake
Scottish accent.

A while back, whilst doing his family tree, Russel had
traced the line of his father back into deep and darkest
Scotland. His once flame-red hair, now grey, had made more
sense to him then. When he told Lou, then the digs and
comments came. Shortbread started appearing. With
random tartan scarfs and hats.

'Funny, Lou. Real funny. For that, you're gettin'
Irish.'

'Jameson's 'll do me grand, Russ son,' Lou said. Both
his grandparents were from over there. So, that made him
half as far as he was concerned.

Russ paused. The wall of fur and trench coats looked
like they were starting to mix, jostle and move a little like
twitching robots with a spill here and shove there.

Yes, the temperature under all those big jackets and
fake hair had definitely risen.

'Two Guinness and two Jameson's please,' Russ got
out before the smash. An arm by him was gripped by a furry
clump. Stuck in a stalemate standing wrestle in a tight space
between pillar and bar the two foes nudging back and forth.
A pint was knocked and another elbowed more forcefully;
sent flying to smash on the floor behind the bar. Like a
storm, the visual smash and scatter seemed to come before
the sound of breaking glass.

The barmaid put Russ's drinks down then shouted
for help, 'Jerry, it's about to kick off. How's about you and
the boy's throw some water on these bears, old ladies jackets

or whatever and those trench coats — cool them down a bit?'

It was too late. The factions meant business. They weren't there to watch Bristol City lose again or whichever horse just fell being put down for not getting up, on-screen.

A stool was picked up. Someone's plate of food was thrown. A table toppled. Arms, heads, legs, and limbs fleyed as Russ quietly ducked, picked up his drinks, and calmly walked a step at a time towards Lou who looked back at Russ in pure ore.

He loved him. The war had never left them. It surrounded them in everything they did. Even now as Russ, a frail old man to some, walked through a bar fight seeming to be protected by an invisible shield. That was war. The Nazi's didn't take him. Now, a load of meat-heads wearing old ladies fur coats and idiots in trench coats couldn't either.

The man was a legend. And Lou decided, when Ross got back to the table he was going to tell him just that. He didn't tell him enough. Now was the time.

He watched Russ's ever so calmly, Buddha-like stroll with his four drinks through a whirlwind of chaos about him. A full-on Western brawl erupted and Russ didn't spill a drop. A light fitting above Russ's head was hit and smashed. As if wearing a forcefield all the bits scattered around, missing him and the drinks. Each step seemed in slow motion. A bear wrestled past with a trench coat-wearing man in a headlock. The bear used the trench coat's head to open the door and they both went falling outside. One of their faces taking the pavement's blow.

Still, Russ didn't spill a drop.

The sirens arrived as Russ put the drinks down. In comedy timing the fur and trench coats dispersed, running off in different directions out of the nearest exits.

'I love you, old man,' Lou said taking a huge gulp of

Guinness. 'Calm under fire. Pure gold. I wish we were in the same service.'

'You wouldn't have made it, Lou.'

Why's that, old man?'

'I'd have had to throw you overboard. Or out a plane at some point… You're a right royal pain in the ass.'

Lou cracked up and hit his hand on the table as two uniforms coasted in, two minutes too late.

'Oh, I nearly forgot… Oh, I've rushed the buggers now,' Russ said, eased his back up and took a packet of salt n' vinegar from his back pocket.

'For that,' Lou said picking the label from a discarded bottle of Heineken, 'I'm going to award you the Red Star Medal, for services in here,' and he waved a hand around at the broken furniture, sparking light fittings and up-tailed pints dripping off the bar, 'in getting us these,' and he gestured to the drinks as crisps on the table.

'Blow it out your arse, Lou. I'll pick the next place.'

Eighteen

PAT AND THE BRISTOL MOB did everything to hold Ballard up. An abandoned transit on the M4 by the Bristol junction created an almighty tailback. They felt guilty for all the others that got stuck with him. But, it had to be done. As Ballard was being held up and pissing in bottles, Pat got to Weston to survey the lay of the land. To see exactly what the fuss was about.

Pat's lads had something a little special for the last hold-up planned. Road sign name changes. Printed and stuck over at key points before and after the Seven Bridge. A bridge Ballard, normally, wouldn't have gone over.

***

Max's black Merc crawled down the seafront slow and menacing and pulled up outside the Weston Fish Bar. It brought black clouds and a change of weather.

He got out the driver side as one of the brothers opened his door. Their look of surprise at Max driving himself was clear on their faces but none of them said a word. Max always had the first word. And the last was his most of all.

'Might have something for you to take care of...in the boot,' Max said.

'Okay, sir,' The Narrator said and his brother, The Echo, moved towards the back of the car.

'Not yet Freakshow number two,' Max muttered, but they all heard. 'The boy's got some hard thinking to do. Let him stew first.'

An hour earlier Max had woken in the back of the

car. He'd been dreaming of what he was going to do to Jimi and Jack. It basically involved a motorboat, a rope, and a jetty. He was going to draw them out real slow at first. Then let the engine open up and rip them in two for the fish to feed on. It was just getting to the tasty, good bit when he woke up.

They were parked up in a town and Danny was reaching back from the driver's seat. Opening Max's jacket. Max's eyes came to. Looking outside, then to Danny's fumbling hand, was he going for the gun?

'What you doing, son? Do you wanna piss left-handed for the rest of your life?'

'Sorry, sir. Was just trying to wake you. It says Weston on the sign. And did pointing us here. But the at Sat Nav says...'

'Why am I seeing, and reading fucking Welsh, boyo?'

'Erghh...'

'Out. NOW!' Max had Danny out, bent over on the floor and hogtied in what seemed like seconds. The bystanders and people shopping in Newport thought nothing of it. Nothing too out of the ordinary for them.

'Sir, I, I... I,' and then he gave up trying to speak. The carpet tape went over his mouth and Max had him launched into the boot. He saw a flash of the holster holding the gun he tried so timidly to take. What if he'd got it, and the table was turned, Danny thought, Max would have been the one in the boot. And this would all be over with. He could have left him in Asda car park and disappeared. Gone. Back to reality rather than being stuck in this nightmare.

'The next time this opens up, son, it'll be your reckoning,' and Max, and shut the lid over Danny's eyes. They'd glossed over, given up. He didn't want this shit. He was no good at it and he was in way over his head.

It wasn't unusual for Max to lose it with his driver.

None of the Cricketers would volunteer for the role. It had the highest turnaround and churn of all their 'field positions'. He was a control freak but insisted on being driven. It was always going to be a tense drive; for the driver most of all.

They didn't ask what was in the boot, they knew already.

'Pat's here,' The Narrator said.

'Well, there's a fucking surprise. I notice *he* didn't get stuck in traffic.'

They pointed at a greasy spoon diner and Max put his hand inside his jacket, touching his piece. It didn't know if he'd need it seeing Pat. But, like a condom, he'd rather have it and not need it, than need it and not have it. He'd told all the others to travel light, to avoid any heavy attention or repercussions. Max obeyed his own rules. And he wasn't going to get caught short by some straw chewing hick in a greasy spoon in Weston.

Max walked over like a bad storm. Opened the door which rang for the girl at the counter to look up, giving a drop of lacklustre attention to the new custom. Booker T and the MG's *Green Onions* played from a jukebox as worn and tired as the rest of the 50s themed diner. He strolled over and slid into the slippery booth seat. It had been polished by chip fat and years of sweat and sea covered arses.

They both stared. Max's eyes hadn't shifted all the way as he'd walked from across the street. Like heat-seekers, on target.

Coffees arrived and still, they remained unmoved.

Pat's black t-shirt clung to him over a bulk of muscle and two layers of cider fat. Max went to take off his black jacket. His own sweat had soaked through the white cotton shirt underneath and his pits needed air. He got as far as flashing the holster and changed his mind. Making out in his face as though it was intentional, that he wanted Pat to know he was carrying.

Pat looked out the window, unperturbed. He had himself covered. He'd met him a few times. Heard about him often and thought about him every second since they'd spoken on the phone. Max made an impression. Like a T-Rex with an M60. And that was just his mouth.

'So, Pat. What brings you here? Thought this wasn't your patch. Looked after itself. Like the Wild West and then some… Isn't that what you said?'

Pat stirred his coffee, added three sugars and stirred slowly again. 'Jimi,' he said and let the name float in the air waiting for Max's vicious tongue to strike out and grab it.

'Jack,' Max said, and let that name hang around too. Floating together in front of two ancient monsters that could eat them like flies.

Both Pat's eyes and a brow raised to gesture. His mouth didn't move.

Both stayed like that for some time, sipping. Pondering. Titans face to face unflinchingly and not wanting to give too much away too early. Life had been both hard and good to both men. To an extent, they were a mirror image: bald heads, deep lines and creases mixed with healed cuts. Well worn faces, travel and weather-beaten, tainted and scarred by the occasional altercation. Tans, so deep it was like they were ex-pats on the Algarve. Or, had worked outdoors most of their lives. But the eyes were where the differences lay. Both sets were hard. Pat's fixed: wise, and laid-back. Like a puma resting in a branch waiting to spring to life and pounce. Max's were a quandary of evil: both dead and manic at the same time. How a white shark might sleep. Eye's open, teeth razor sharp. Even at rest: savage.

'You know what sleep deprivation does to a person, Pat? Why Guantanamo uses it…? The SAS train to battle it. Knowing they'll face if they're caught by the enemy… It changes you, Pat. Rewires your thinking processes. '

Pat looked out the window and back again. He was ready for a speech. The hardest thing was trying not to yawn.

'I met a girl once... Nice lass. We were both on our arses, having a hard time you could say. She was down, in a dark place. I'm always there, sometimes the light just goes out altogether. Anyway, I met this girl. We hit off. In The Black Sheep in Oval, been there, Pat?'

'Heard about it.'

'Thing is, two people normally not meant to meet and hit it off like that, but, when one's rewired like that, temporarily put onto your darker wavelengths... Well, we did, we hit it off. She hadn't slept in months, maybe a year. If you saw into her eyes, you could see that her soul had dropped out. She'd given herself over wholeheartedly to feed, care and look after her child. A son, Pat.'

'Who?'

'Patience, Pat.'

'Someone once told me there's a tribe in the Amazon. They've an unorthodox way of getting the little boys to sleep at night. The mothers will do anything. Well... you can imagine, Pat... Makes you wonder who was the first to try it. So, by now it's so commonplace and they think it's their daily *kind of normal.*'

Pat felt sick. At what Ballard was saying and how he was delivering it: cold, plain, so matter of fact. He knew Ballard had a thing for winding people up before engaging fully. Liked to see them squirm, then to be as full of adrenaline as he was. Pat didn't rise to it. He looked out the window calmly again and then back at Max. Then, he started his counterattack, with a serene blankness to cancel him out.

Tracey was working the long counter that day. Serving coffee and flipping bacon and eggs into dripping baps. Once a blonde bombshell, now she was a tired husk.

Serving a lifetime of tourists, rude teens and hardened locals had taken a toll. Four kids and a lazy husband had done the rest. Used to serving the fore-mentioned for twenty odd years, day in day out, Pat and Max stood out like two shiny black towers in a desert. Every time she went over to refill them or ask if they wanted to order she could feel a charge in the air. And when she actually stood at the end of their table, pad and pencil in hand, the room damn-near seemed to vibrate. In their dark energy. She leant on her counter staring, transfixed on them.

'Alreet, Trace,' a Geordie, down for a few days said, 'you lookin' to stare them guys down like? I think they're pretty fixed on each other. Three-way staring match doesn't work so good anyhow from a distance.'

Another coffee in and it had almost touched the sides. It was thick, tar-like, and strong. Both men were almost immune. Used to harder pick me ups.

'Max, I respect you,' Pat started. He glanced outside again as a seagull chased a tabloid sheet down the pavement for a lone chip stuck to it. 'I do. But... You are crazy, right?'

Max stared on. Wanted to hear the piece Pat had to say. He thought, maybe that he wasn't as dumb as all that, maybe. Is he coming with some verbal recourse, a counter-offensive? Had it sunk in though, did Pat get what Max was getting to? That all this was by design. Jimi, Jack... Jimi's ex-wife. Jack's mother. It wasn't some random coincidence that Jack should end up here, in Weston. Forced to face up against his own father. Dumb fuck was meant to teach him some manors the hard way, admittedly. Not, fucking befriend the guy. Max had thought it poetic justice at the time. Jimi hadn't been there for his son, had driven his tired wife mad. His mother's brain was unable to care and comfort Jack so...he'd ended up the way he did. Futureless but for a life on the street working for the likes of Max. He'd seen him trying to get his attention for a while, knew who he was. By the time he bashed that irritating tourist yammering over the game, Max had already decided what was to happen.

Max had been seeing Jack's mother on the side. During his *darker* times. He hated Jimi, for what she said he did to her. He used Jack. A chip of the block, he just saw him as another drain on her. He was damaged goods now too, so why not fix them both, he'd thought.

'You are crazy...right? I mean you see the world differently from everyone else. Puts you in good stead for your line of work, and where you're doing it: that big bastard city. Times have changed though, Max, and this isn't the big smoke,' and he put a smartphone on the table. It was Face-Timing. The people at the other end had been listening in and now, they could see too. 'Don't mind if they join us do they?' and he propped Jimi and Jack up against the sugar shaker and ketchup.

Max Ballard's arrogant self-assured comfort zone was wavering. Pat could see a twitch of his eyelid. It was enough. If it was a poker he'd know he had him.

'Max,' Jimi said from the phone. 'I did everything for her, my wife.'

'Butt out for now, Jimi. This isn't about you, yet,' Pat said. All the words being used had been around Jimi, Jack, and Max's part-time ominous cross over into stepdad of Jack. But, Pat knew, Max had bigger beef — there was something else. He didn't believe he drove all the way here just to plug a retired builder who walked out on his wife. He'd be busy in Weston if he did. There weren't enough bullets for that. No, Max had a chip, a gripe. 'What's the real issue here, Max? Save of face? Pride dented. I don't believe you were ever that into her. Not anyone. It's not your style. People are casual throwaway items. Other than your own, close at heart, her indoors. Where is she actually now, Max?

In some skiing chalet with her pals?'

'Don't go there, Pat,' and Max's hand twitched, jerked towards his inner jacket.

'I mean good here, Max,' Pat said and put a hand under the table. 'I mean, at heart: you have got one. This hard man gangster shit is your shop. A facade. We're a little more down to earth over here, Max. You don't need to come over all heavy. What's the real steak here?'

Max stared hard and long. Pat almost thought he saw a tear. But, as soon as the notion surfaced it was gone. An illusion of emotion in the old beast. Now he looked out the window, then to the phone with Jack and Jimi on, and then back to Pat.

'What you really want, Max?'

'You ever heard of Ian Banks?'

'No, Max.'

'He had this bar in Soho: The Barfly. Great place. Sweat dripped down the walls, the bands rocked every night. I saw The Clash there. The guys dripped with sweat and the girls were wet for it too. I miss that place,' Jimi sat up on-screen — Max was speaking his language now. 'Ian ran that place like a machine. He was one of *us* too but he kept control of his certain field, and within safe perimeters, you might say. His comfort zone was well defined. Simple really. The travelling support bands that gigged there would come from all over, they'd turn up with two or three extra guitar and gig cases full of merch' going to and fro. Yeah, real simple. In fact, most of it was sold to the customers watching the bands, the bands themselves and the staff. So it never left the four grubby walls after it arrived. Yeah, I loved that place, loved Ian too.'

'What happened, Max?'

'I got carried away. Forgot how much it worked with him as part of the chemistry. I just saw the success of it. So

I wanted the place badly. Took it. It didn't work though. And we fell out over that and a few other things… They're still picking bits of him out of the river by the South Bank.'

'What's the point, Max? You want a bar. A gig venue? Is that why you sent that the brothers in to get their youngest to play. Was that your way of leveraging in?'

'Wasn't on my mind. Guess the subconscious and the gut instinct win out a lot of the time though,' Max said. 'And now it has won over… I thought I wanted it there, in London. Now I've seen the place. It's here.'

'You've just arrived, Max, walked twenty paces.'

'Doesn't matter, you get a feel for a place. A town — I want it. And most of all, I want The Hell's Belles.'

The phone on the table went dead. Jimi shut the call down.

Nineteen

HE OUTBOARD MOTORS rattled away as the sea did its work; cleansing, making good, calming their insides as the saltwater repaired bruises, cuts and battered skin. Jack and Jimi faced the island. The crews looked across at them from another boat.

'Just let him have it,' Jack said against the wind. He meant the bar but didn't mind if Jimi took it any other way.

'It won't end at the bar, son. That guy's quite a big fish for Weston's tiny waters.'

'He's a fucking maniac.'

'Some people say the same about me.'

'Seriously... just let him have it.'

'It's his to take now, isn't it? With no one there to watch over her. It's not *that* I'm worried about. Not anymore.'

'What then?'

'Well, look how all green-eyed and greedy he got about our spit and sawdust den: The Belles,' Jimi said as they touched the shore. 'What do you think he'll make of all this? A real-life, ready-made gangsters paradise,' and he opened his arms as if to embrace the entire island.

Betty and Tammy looked out from the inn on the rocky slope up ahead. Jack smiled at the girls and the work they'd done. Both Jimi and Jack's confidence was dented by Max Ballard's arrival. As their feet sunk into the shingle their morale followed. Looking up, Betty and Tammy looked hard, strong. And in a glance, they seemed to repair both men before either had started the ascent.

'Let him fucking try,' Jack said.

'Aye. And he will. Have no doubt, son. He will.'

***

'You could have just asked, Max — why go carrying on, creating this mess,' Pat said in the diner as the jukebox played B. B. King's, *The Thrill is Gone*.

'Yeah, like you said: crazy... aren't I.'

'Jimi's a good lad. He's straight. Not one of us. A fucking retired builder with a retirement plan. All he wants to do is drink Jack D and play his guitar.'

'What's he got over you, Pat. Why you go giving a flying fuck?' Max didn't raise his voice. He didn't have to.

'He did some time for us. Was mistaken for one of my drivers in a line-up. He knew who we were and who they were after — kept it shut. That same driver has gone on to be a bit of a high rolling cash cow since.'

'Good for you. Could do with a good driver. Maybe I'll take *him* too. Just had to give my current one the boot!' Max grunted a restrained laugh. Outside the brothers waved at Max and he gave them the thumbs up. Pat looked out to see them pull the heap of a man from the back of Max's car.

'Another work experience lad gone bad, Max? For fuck's sake. Your people skills leave a lot to be desired. You know they're important for running a place.'

Max wasn't listening, his mind had moved on. 'Right, enough of this small talk. Finish up. You're showing me my new bar. And it better be close by.'

Pat kept his strength. Didn't give in to Max's attempt to override and control him. He knew Max would take The Belles if he was meant on it. And, at the end of the day, it wasn't Pat's to protect. Pat's little catch-up with Max had been planned, and two-fold: to get under Max's skin, find out what was pushing him here. And, to buy Jimi and Jack some time for a getaway. And... Pat had something else up his sleeve. A wildcard. Pat knew who Jimi's brother was: John Black. Black was an ex-SAS and a police informant. On a recent undercover police mission, he toppled the *Mr Big* of Manchester's gangland... Somehow ending up both revered by the police and the toughest Manchester gangs. And to top it all he'd written it all out in his latest book. His name and actions had become legend. Ballard hadn't joined the dots. But Pat had...long ago. He didn't let slip much to Jimi — made out like he was just paying a debt back to him for keeping his mouth shut. Pat knew there'd come a time when knowing his brother could be leverage. Toppling Ballard was such a time and a necessity.

Cream's *Sunshine of Your Love* played as they both stood up. A loud Velcro ripping noise cut through the music and made Ballard stare at Pat. Pat casually took the .38 snub nose he'd had stuck to the underside of the table and put it away. Smooth and laid back, like he was pocketing a packet of cigarettes. He wanted Max to notice. He eased the hammer back down back into place first. He wanted Max to see that too, and to know at the time Max had been playing Billy Big Balls and gesturing to his jacket, all the while the hammer was back and ready to do him.

Max nodded respect. He was impressed. And that wasn't easy these days.

Clapton's solo played as they walked to the door. Its overhead bell rang as it opened, flooding the diner with gull sounds from outside. Another ring signalled the door shutting.

Tracey hadn't moved. Eyes fixed on them from the counter. Her one other customer had been and gone. She felt for a moment that life that had been breathed into the place, and her. In the time Pat and Max were there the place had become somehow... significant. She came to, sedated back into her reality, poured a coffee, picked up her fags and went out back for a smoke by the tubs of solidified cooker fat she'd left out overnight. Every night. It went hard, like lard. The stray cats liked licking it. She hadn't had any complaints from the customers about a slight taste of cat or cigarette ash. This was her moment of respite; coffee and a fag. A break and backlash against the place. Set in ash and those butts put out in the dirty old fat. The cats licked around the fag butts to get to the recycled bacon fat. Everything in that town found a way around the unpleasantness to get what they needed to get by.

***

Max's wife's condition took both of them by surprise — out of the blue. 'I don't feel so good' turned into 'I'm a bit dizzy and need a lie down' by a day or two. Within a space of a month, she didn't leave the bed at all. They'd held back from contacting the doctor, not wanting to waste anyone's time with a bit of: 'under the weather'. By the time they relented it was too late.

That's how Max met Jimi's wife. They were both in a dark place. Despair had wrapped itself around every aspect of their being. As Max had leant against the bar of The Black Sheep drinking through the disbelief that his wife, so young, was being taken by an incurable Big C, he was hollow inside. Jimi's wife was similar in vacated emotion and reasoning. But over a different sort of life's punishment. She hadn't slept in months and saw no support or change up ahead. A friend had insisted she took her son for a while… So she could clear her head. And that's when she met Max Ballard.

Max had three empty tumblers in front of him on the bar. Jimi's ex-wife had one, full and untouched. The vacuum they created between them had drawn any atmosphere from the place and pulled them together. They grew closer, although saying nothing. Her friend, realising her son was at risk, that she would lose him to Social Services if it kept up, took him more and more. And it went on like that for weeks. By the time Max's wife had died Jimi had been kicked out and their son stayed with that friend semi-permanently.

Her glass wasn't un-touched anymore and Max's number of empties had grown too.

'Where'd he go? This so-called husband: Jimi.'

'He was never there, to begin with... Providing for us, he used to say. Could have done with less of the little money he brought in. More nappy changes, instead. And a break for me. Bounced from Bristol to Weston-super-Mare last I heard. His cheques still come. Small, but they do come...'

'Modern man,' Max said. It was both a question and comment on what it is to be one.

'Not much of that in this part of the world,' she said.

After spending the night together they agreed the boy would never find out. It was a temporary comfort; pleasure out of pain for them both. Not meant to last. But not to be underestimated either. Two people not usually meant to be together, closer than ever in an explosion of hurt. He wanted her to get back on her feet. He didn't want the boy getting close to someone new only for them to leave. He knew the drill. Paid his way and made sure she was never without. From then on his eyes and mind sought a way to make it right. For the opportunity.

'See you on the other side,' Max said during their last goodbye.

'Thank you,' she said and she meant it, 'for saving me.'

She picked up her son from her friend's flat and held on to him. The friend looked on as they walked away. Fear and worry for the boy filled her face. She'd smelt the whiskey on her breath when she opened the door. And she'd also heard she been seen in The Black Sheep with Max Ballard; a crook's crook. And big-time bad news for her and the boy.

The friend wasn't religious. That night she said a prayer for the boy anyway. The nightly sirens drowned out any chance of her being heard.

By the time Jack hit that tourist in The Black Sheep to impress Max Ballard, his fate had already been set in motion. Like mercury pooling together, everyone's destiny fused as one.

***

Max thought about renaming Jimi's bar 'Howzat', as a fingers up to him; a perfect gesture from The South Bank Cricketers. He nearly named it 'Enter Sandman's' as a musical overwrite of The Hell's Belles name too. He fancied Metallica over ACDC and thought it would sufficiently rub Jimi's nose in it all the more. In the end, he went for straight forward simplicity: 'The Cricketers Arms'. The sign had a crossed cricket bat and rifle — it did what it said on the tin. Simple, hard, straight forward. How he saw himself.

Despite, or because of this, Max's new bar was dead — literally not a soul in there. In Jimi's hands, you could hardly move for sweaty backs, shoulders and arms as condensation clung to the windows. And it was like that from opening 'till closing time. Now it was a ghost town. Max's ego couldn't take it, three days in and he wanted income aside from the usual skimming, hustling and scams he had the crews working. So far his retirement plan wasn't making enough to make the rent. Like he intended paying it. As far as he was concerned it was his.

A few punters, one or two, walked in, then straight back out again when they saw Max's steely face behind the bar. On leaving they looked up, saw the sign, nodded as if to say 'ah change of hands', then walked. A few steps down the alley and their nods turned to head shakes. In knowing they'd have to find somewhere else for a fix. Weston was short of the atmosphere Jimi brought with the Belles. He had provided a much needed public service and a means of letting off steam. Max had unknowingly robbed the town of it. Without a finger on the town's pulse or experience of pulling pints or playing to a sweaty crowd. It was missing an elusive x-factor, out of reach... And he wanted it bad.

'What's with this place? Why don't they come in, and drink some?' Max said to an empty room.

The door opened with a creak as Pat and five of his Bristol mob walked in: two women and three men.

'Thought you could do with some customers, Max.'

'Seriously, where the fuck is everyone?' Max said. He wasn't defeated, Pat could still see cast iron determined stubbornness in his eyes. He wouldn't give up. Men like him didn't. Leaders of men.

'There's enough dead-end boozers in this town. Why do you have to go creating another one? It's lacking soul, Max. Like the new landlord,' Pat winked and Max ignored him. He was stuck in a loop. Three days was too long, he was impatient, and wanted instant success. Max was the same in school when he turned up. It would have taken too long to attend, toe the line and wait for results before moving on. Max soon realised he could delegate the schoolwork, with a threat or offer of small change. The same small change he'd robbed from the lockers of the kid he got to do the schoolwork for him. It was a simple economic lesson. By the time he had the streets of South London the principles held the same: 'I'm taking from you. If you want it back, I'm going to need something from you worth more.' He'd sell hundreds of pills to waiting punters queuing outside

Madame Jo Jo's nightclub, only to have his associate take it back off them on the door before letting them in. They never learned. By the time they bought another fix inside, they had to pay double. So Max made enough to pay himself, the dealers, and the door staff plenty.

'Why did *he* have it filled up every night?'

'Jimi... He played guitar. Not great. But good enough for *here*. A one-man karaoke rock show. They love that kinda shit over here. Self-deprecating. Not taking themselves too seriously. You should try a drop of that, Max. Loosen up — you might live longer. '

'Fuck that.'

'Then, I guess you'll be off back to the big smoke then?' and Pat wished he would.

'You're forgetting something, Pat.'

'What?'

'It's a *who*. That younger brother that wanted to play in the first place that kicked all this off. The boy Matt.'

'Good luck with that, Max.'

'What d'ya mean?' Max snarled. The suggestion that anything he'd arranged wasn't perfect had his hackles high. Pat could see it and toned down the wind-up. Pat was a lesser peer in Max's eyes. Pat could get away with only so much. Pat saw himself as an equal. Max, however, only saw himself equal to God and the Devil.

'Like I said. Jimi was a one-man rock show. Rough around the edges. They kinda like that… Matt's… well… too polished. Cheese-fest.'

'He'll fucking blow the lid off, Pat.'

'A tin of candy floss and soda piss,' Pat muttered under his breath, and he and the rest drank up and left.

'Ain't you forgetting something, fuckers!' Max yelled down the street as the veins bulged on his neck with the scream. The blood ran pulsing up and over his bald head.

'Add it to my slate,' Pat shouted without turning, 'it's behind the bar. Marked Pat's Cider fund!'

Max thought about barring them. But there was no one to make the example too. He needed the customers, even if they were scrumpy swigging gangsters like Pat. And he could kid himself that this bar would be his clean break, but that shit didn't come off. The history.

As Pat and his crew discussed if Max would ever leave or give in chasing Jimi now he had the bar, Max waited for his new entertainment to arrive...he said 5.30 pm sharp to Matt and it wasn't 5.15 yet. Max wanted everyone to be half an hour early. This applied to everything. Being on time wasn't enough. You had to have turned up eager and have waited to be graced with max's presence. It's just the way it is.

They blew open and in walked Matt, slowly squeaking. His tight shiny white leather jumpsuit with red lighting flashes clung to every inch of his now paunchy frame. He had the sweat on him of a grand national winners arse, and he hadn't even started yet. He was eager. And had spent the best bit of the bay preening and prancing only to sweat through it all. He panted in anticipation and after the rush up the cobbles. His Cuban heels had clacked all the way as his flight case pulled on his hand.

'What the fuck have you come as son, a walking coke can?'

'Sorry I'm early... but late. The others said: be early or else.'

'Didn't say how early did they? There'd be an *or else*, but I don't have *anyone else*. Now, get plugged in son. Let them know we're here.'

'When's the rest turning up?'

'Who?'

'The band?'

Max's heart sank and his temper rose. 'Jimi played the shit out of this place on his own... What do you need? I thought your brothers said you were good... Now play!'

Matt's big break had turned like Max's previous driver after the first road turning. It had all gone sour. He needed to get through the night without being trunked, buried in the sand or floated out to sea. Matt's mother used to say: 'you've got two types of people in this world, Matty. Radiators and drains. Your brothers, unfortunately, are drains. But you, Matty, you are a shining light, a radiator. Don't ever forget that...'

'Yo! PVC Prick! Snap to it, or I'll turn on the jukebox and float you out to sea,' Max's words hit Matt and he shook. His plectrum poised in, he plugged in his all-white Stratocaster as the options of something to play went spinning through his mind, and none of it seemed hard enough for Max.

Twenty

J ACK'S UNMADE PRAYERS had come true. A father. A home. Even some extras: two strong mothers-in-law and an island to themselves. False memories of his dad had been jaded and turned by his resenting mother and he'd grown up unsure where the truth lay between the battered images she lay and enforced for him.

When he was five he thought the man in the room next to his bedroom with his mother *was* his father. She'd make horrible noises, the man too. Screeches, moans, and whimpers. He thought she was in pain as they appeared occasionally in the corridor of their tiny one and a half bed flat, covered in sweat. This man would stumble around, crash into things, shouting. Once he threw their TV out the window to the street below. He smelt of something musty, chemicals and smoke.

After a while, a month or six, Jack stopped knocking on the bedroom door to see if she was alright. A red angry face had appeared to tell him to fuck off and he retreated into his room and himself, wishing the walls were more than thin plasterboard and put a pillow over his head. Even the cat seemed to feel his pain and lay on top of the pillow as an extra layer of insulation.

It was some years later when he realised what the cries were something else, not pained. And that the man wasn't his father.

Once Jack was chased home by a gang of older boys. They wanted Jack to break into a building site with them. Smash stuff up. Climb up really high on scaffolding... Jack's instinct said they wanted to do something to him on that site.

That they meant to hurt him. For him to have an accident. He ran from them, heart pounding as they chased and threw rocks, then he banged on the door to be let back in. The sweaty angry man was there again. Furious at the boy's interruption. His mother stayed in the bedroom like Jack hadn't existed. As if the man had left to answer the door to a postman. At five years old Jack was now that invisible to her. Jack told the angry (drunken) man that there were boys bigger than him and they were trying to get Jack to do stuff that he didn't want to do, and he was scared. Angry man had no time for this. He had a specific window of opportunity to do what he needed to do with Jack's mother between the heavy drinking, necessary to blur images of the Falkland War in his head. Jack shook as the angry man raged on. He grabbed the boy and pulled him down the back stairs to the outhouse. Jack still remembered the sounds of his bare feet on the wooden steps, the dust in the air mixing with the man's sweat. It dripped down his back and over scars and a tattoo of knives and snakes weaving together with a fusilier regiment's name. The man grabbed and dragged a length of wood, a hammer, some six-inch nails and threw Jack to the floor. Jack had already realised he was more scared of the angry man than the older boys. But he was stuck in a vortex. From that he'd learned: when in trouble, or scared, never go back home — don't go running to mum. The man laid the length of wood across a log and picked up the first nail. In a flash, he'd manically battered it in with the hammer. One stroke: bang. Then another one was in, and another. They poked through the plank making some medieval-looking weapon — crooked crocodile's teeth. Much more dangerous than a building site. Jack attempted to cower away, head in arms, but the man didn't give him a choice. He told him to take it and batter the biggest boy in the group, forced into his little hand that could barely hold the weight. If that didn't make them run, then he was told to take out the next biggest one. Go for the knees and shins he told him. And then his hairy sweaty back turned and he disappeared behind a slammed shack of a door.

Another time Jack found the angry man sat on the floor in front of the coal fire. Again, shirt off and sweating. His mother had asked him why he had to do *that* in there. Jack wasn't sure what she meant. As he got closer he saw the man had a Bowie knife in the fire. His bare feet were up on the hearth as he played with a nail on his right foot. The little one next to his big toe. He seemed to prod, pick, and inspect it. Then he took the blade from the fire...and then there was blood. It came from his toe as he cut into it, releasing a long-ignored ingrown nail. The man seemed oblivious to the pain. And the boy stared entranced by the blood, flames, and the man's trance-like disregard for his own body. He looked over to his mother in the small kitchenette who was equally disconnected from him, the man, and the goings-on.

It hurt Jack to tell Betty and Tammy the memories, purging himself — making it clear some of where he'd come from. They looked at him and at each other; ashamed for motherhood. And when they told Jimi, he felt ashamed for fatherhood. The mess of an absent father, broken present mother and the influence on a child was now in front of them. They saw strength in him despite this. And in a chink of their glasses felt pride being with him. As he was them. The sounds of the waves caressed the outside of the inn. None of them had had an easy ride to be there. Everyone had baggage.

'How long before this Max guy figures where we are?' Betty said as the moonlight reflected off her jet-black hair.

'He'll spend a few days establishing himself. Overriding the memory of our place in the town...'

'Look, Jimi,' Tammy said pointing to the laptop on the bar. It showed the CCTV footage of the front of Jimi's bar. A man in a white jumpsuit stumbled in carrying a guitar case. Max's hands grabbed and drag him in.

'Oh, this is gonna be good.'

'What d'you mean, Jimi?' Jack said.

'Well, I'm betting this is going to be the most interesting case of watching paint dry we ever had... Pour us a round, son, and let's enjoy it.'

They watched on as nothing happened. Then one customer walked in, then out again. Then two tourists, then out again. It went on like that for an hour. The guy in the jumpsuit was seen dragging his amp and guitar onto the cobbles outside.

'That was my trick to get them in at first. It ain't gonna work with any of the pop ballard 80's shite that prat belts out though.'

A few minutes later and the brothers turned up to support their youngest.

'A bit late for that aren't they. And where's the rest of them?' Jack said.

Then they appeared; a huddle of trench coats. Some tracksuits lurked in the corner of the camera shot, sniggering, and nudging each other. One of them picked up a bottle from by their feet and threw it at Matt's amp. Another threw the can he was swigging from, catching Matt's guitar. Sparks flew. The nepotistic crowd broke and made chase after the tracksuits. Matt struggled to take his guitar off as the sparks flew from him like he was a gay bar crotch grinder. The amp smoked his defeat in the background.

Max's silhouette was unmistakable against the entrance door frame. He looked to the ground, beaten and shook his head.

'Elvis, my sweethearts. Has left the building,' Jimi

laughed. 'And... goodnight!'

'What's that in his hand?' Betty said, getting a closer look.

'What is it?' Jack sounded worried.

'Fuckity fuck,' said Tammy.

'Fuck indeed,' Jimi said when he realised, Max was holding a corner of the map they'd made from sellotaped together A4s.

'I think it's time, Jimi... To show you, Old Rosie,' Betty said.

***

Max was a machine. As the hands of the clock on the wall moved, he barely noticed. Other than the arms occasionally blocking and then revealing different hot spots of Bettie Page's photo beneath. His days and years were measured in self-set milestones. He slept when these had been met; incremental pockets of achievement in his eyes alone. Immune to the irrelevant subjective weight of time, his assignments were a much heavier pressure. They kept him moving always forwards. It was a distraction from the brutality of life's inevitability, after the death of his wife.

The problems came when these markers weren't met. And his patience, and temper, broke whilst waiting for results — forcing him into facing reality and time's march. And reminding him of events and things he didn't want to dwell on for the sake of weakening himself.

The boy Matt was trying this patience hard. He'd played for what felt like hours now, and nothing. He was limp bate, catching nothing. They might as well be rolling turds into burgers and trying to sell them to the passing trade.

'Take your kit, PVC Prick, and set up outside. And turn that fucker up...and for twat's sake play something that rocks.'

Matt dragged at the guitar and amp, all still plugged in. In his haste to get out the door, the cables caught on the door frame and pulled the plugs out of the extension that teetered on the bar. It dropped behind, a glass smashed and Matt froze like a statue. Max didn't. He vaulted the bar like a man half his age all the while eyes fixed, glaring at Matt.

'Get out and play. I'll sort this,' Max said and stooped behind. As he fumbled impatiently between broken glass, water and cables for the extension socket a small sheet of A4 caught his eye.

He plugged the boy in.

Inspecting the damp A4 sheet like it was an artefact, he turned it, unfolded it, held it to the light. He could see it was a map. The significance and place would take a while to drop. But it would...drop. He stepped into the doorway to see a few faces turning up down the alley. Most were familiar; Mat's brother's the rest of Max's Cricketer's mob in trench coats, but there were a few new faces, drawn by the crowd. Matt's cheese-assed rendition of some Bon Jovi crap wasn't right, but it was a step roughly in the right direction.

By the time the sparks had started to fly, the damp sheet of A4 had nearly dried. And with it his thoughts on its significance. The bar had taken a back seat. The boy could keep hammering away, getting that off the ground. Playing until his fingertips bled. Now, Max had Jimi back in his sights. The itch needed scratching. The milestone to be made rubble before Max could move on.

**

Old Rosie was four Northumbrian fish Coble boats bolted together. She had four outboard motors to the back, black sails and a washed-up old mannequin fixed to a plank between the front two boats. Under the water were two hidden battering rams. Makeshift harpoons with rods and rags dipped in diesel armed port and starboard whilst a pirate black flew overhead. When Jimi saw her that night, the boy in him woke again, like the first strum on his SG. It was pure divine magic — crafted by ancient women Norse gods that were Betty and Tammy.

Jack's mouth dropped open and Jimi couldn't stop smiling. As the moon caught the waves all their minds were taken deep into their heritage. As Jimi touched the craft he felt electricity, power, and the relentless power of the sea.

'This isn't your war anymore, Jimi,' Tammy said.

'It's ours,' Betty added. And in a crack of lighting overhead the two men shrank as the Viking goddesses held the reins. Their ebony and blonde hair silhouetted in the next crash of lighting and Jimi and Jack swore they saw something else. The women had become the island, the boat, and the sea.

'God help Max and the Cricketers,' Jack muttered.

'Better warn Pat and the Bristol boys too. To stay out the way,' Jimi said.

Twenty-One

'I T'S AN ISLAND. WHAT MORE CAN I SAY?'
The bar around Max and Pat darkened, creaking with the tension behind Max's eyes as he listened to Pat. He saw through him. Felt he'd helped Jimi get away. Unsure of something though. Max wasn't feeling the usual need to push hard... to a breaking point. Something in his gut stopped him before he made an enemy of him too. For now.

'You don't know any more about it then...why this piece of map is here, in Jimi's old place. And where this island is?' Max's voice was flat, no aggression, matter of fact. His finger tapped at the bedraggled stained sheet like a bus conductor waiting for proof of a ticket. It was Pat's virtual ticket. His chance of acceptance at taking clear sides in the fight. To side with Max and give up Jimi.

'Look past the pier, next time you let yourself out. You'll see two lumps of land in the sea. It's the one on the left: Steep Holm. Nothing much has been going on there in donkey's years,' Pat saw no point in being totally obstructive. Max wasn't stupid. And the symbolic fence Pat and his crew were sat on was collapsing all the time.

Max knew Pat's loyalties were strong with Jimi. 'If I asked you if Jimi's is held up there on that lump of rock, and that you bought him time to get there... I wonder where we'd be, Pat?' There was a symmetry to Max's emotions. A furious rage and an animalistic attacking force balanced by a calm zen-like composure. At any point, the chemistry and weight of his making could tip the balance.

For now, something deep, a gut instinct, kept his calm.

He knew Pat had helped Jimi. For now, that

knowledge was enough, without action. Max's fuse was lit though and it wouldn't dampen. Not for all the murky waters in the Bristol Channel.

'I reckon if we went down that route, Jimi wouldn't get that chance to face up to you, Max. Most likely he wouldn't see me again either,' Pat muttered and tapped the bulge of his .38 under his belt. In the background of the bar, both their crews firmed up too. Hands went into pockets. Staring down their equals in the opposing crew's ranks. Really, it was an admittance of a stalemate but showing they'd take the risk anyway. That was enough to show max. That they still were meant, had bottle, were peers cut from the same cloth.

'There's a second island, Max,' Pat said. 'If you just want whatever he's got, just take that. You have the bar already,' and with that, he'd answered Max: he knew where Jimi was.

'Thanks, Pat, but I'm staying in town. In a month it'll all be mine. And the fucking islands.'

'Didn't have you down as greedy, Max,' Pat didn't mean it. He could see Max hadn't had his fill, wasn't going to stop. Pat needed to tip the favour of the battle whilst still vaguely one-sided. Taking a side against Max and the South Bank Cricketers, out in the open, would be professional, and possible, actual suicide.

Pat knew now he was going to have to throw a wildcard into the mix. He was going to have to ring Jimi's estranged brother: John Black. The ex-SAS, police informant and Manchester gang overlord… It would be risky. Worst of all everything that happened would end up in one of his sodding books — they'd all be exposed.

The realisation dropped. This was right, get it done and they'd all have to retire, including Max. No more skirting around the issue. They were getting on. Long in the tooth and nothing to show for it but a few scars and reputation.

Pat gulped at his Thatchers Gold and tasted nothing. Then, he sipped again and tasted every crushed apple and hand that had touched their skins, the sun that ripened them, and the soil that bore the trees they'd grown on... The prospect of retirement had awakened possibilities of a new easy life. One that he hadn't thought would happen. He could smell the Somerset country air and feel the grass beneath his feet. He was right there, his toes tickled by damp grass underfoot.

'You ever gonna lay the tools down, Max? Call it a day... Times have changed. Let these new lads 'n lasses take over.'

'If I stop moving, pushing, having a go — even worse, forget letting some fucking builder and his son walked all over me, I'll start *remembering*. And I... don't want that. I'm like those couples you see on holiday, rather than sunbathing and taking it easy they have to be *Doing shit*: Exploring. Discovering. Always on the move. Everyone else takes it easy, sips on a cocktail, catches rays and finishes a Jilly Cooper or Fifty Shades of Shit. Whilst they're walking five miles to a local market. Then, hike ten bastard miles the wrong way to take in some sightseeing,' Max's words painted pictures of him and his wife, happily in flux, constantly jostling and moving together, never apart. 'I need to be actioning...*doing*, Pat... I don't want to *remember*,' Max looked solemn and tainted. Like a grave with wilted flowers being pissed on by a passing terrier. 'Besides, you know what happens when those couples do try to be like everyone else and take it easy...and just lay about? They fucking fight. Faced with the realities of their own company, they're like cat and dog. Ripping at each other's throats...'

'At least think about it, Max, just *think* about it,' Pat finished up and walked his crew out. He knew Max wouldn't *think* about anything. Other than his next move. He wouldn't stop. The ghost of his wife was waiting to pop out of her casket if he ever did.

Pat was going to have to make that call. And they'd all retire or die. Either way, they'd end up in *that* book, exposed. The whole caper was rapidly turning into a Weston-super-Nightmare. And there wouldn't be a sequel.

***

John Black began life as a mistake. A misplaced seed drunkenly spilt and planted at a party his parents had crashed. By the time the cushions they were buried in had parted, and his parents stumbled out, the two teens had altered theirs and their future children's fates forever. John's father didn't hang around to be berated for the blame. And by the time a second son arrived, Jimi, *that* father didn't hang around either. Their mother carried the tiredness of two children and the baggage of abandonment at the hardest time when she needed support the most. So, half-brothers, Jimi and John were no more bonded than they were to their mother. A three-way mistake jostling about, making no sense of it. Never seeking comfort in what was in front because it reminded them of what, and who had left them behind.

They survived long enough, then flew the nest. Emotionally hardened through a childhood distancing, despite the tiny flat they all shared. They both sought family and belonging elsewhere. John's came from the army. Jimi's in the comradery of building sites. There was no real bad blood between them. Just the half-blood they'd shared was diluted by a bitter mother's resentment of both their absent fathers.

John refused to shoot back in Ireland and saw ghosts of his heritage in the flames of war. He was discharged. He still saw the same ghosts when he worked the doors of the clubs in Manchester. He fell in deep with the gangs but some innate cell in him, like with Jimi, kept him ultimately always wanting to do the right thing — to correct a past they had no control over. And after a girl died from a bad pill in the club John worked the doors of, he stuck his neck out and testified against the gangs' overlord: Mr Big. Destiny, fate, and heritage pulled at him. Fast forward a bit and he was somehow revered by the gangs and the police.

John was a hard act to follow. Jimi kept his distance, following his brother in the news and read the blurb on the back of his books. He made his own way. Proud to get his hands dirty another way. Maybe that's why Jimi fell in with Pat and his crew in The Cornubia. As Jimi's subconscious drew him near to those criminals similar to those of his brother's world.

When the call came from Pat, John was walking along a stretch of beach in Northumberland. He hadn't felt a need to go back since doing service. A funeral felt reason enough. To forget the past, to make the journey. But remembering enough to pay respects.

The morning's crisp sand broke as the surface crust broke under his feet. Dunes swept up and over him to the right as the North Sea attacked old wooden breaks to the left. They didn't stand a chance.

'I was trying to forget family whilst I was here.'

'He needs help. We *all* do.'

'Okay, Pat.'

'DON'T kill him, John. Don't... Kill... Ballard.'

'I'll leave that for Jimi to decide. There might not be an option. Max Ballard might not have heard of me, yet. But I have him.'

'John...'

'Yes, Pat.'

'When you write it up. Can you make me younger, with hair and harder than Ballard?'

'Click,' and John left, returning to the sounds of the white horses crashing at his feet. The sea spray hit his face as he stood resolute as an ancient statue washed over my rising sea levels. He turned to face the sea and saw Vikings. A glorious fleet of fierce women and men that wouldn't back down. Not ever.

He could afford an overnighter. The bodies would still be cold when he returned.

Twenty-Two

THE CREWS ON THE ISLAND BRACED for a storm and an attack by the Cricketers gang.

'Anything yet?' Tammy asked, getting her kit together.

Jack, Jimi, Betty, and Tammy had been glued to the CCTV footage all morning. The midday sun was nearing and they could finally stop squinting from it streaming through the cracks in the old windows' shutters. They flicked the footage from outside Max's bar, to the landing zones on the shores. Any activity or flurry of trench coats to the ores and they were poised, ready.

Clouds shifted. The sky started to change, black.

Jack turned and knocked a glass to the floor. They all jumped and for the first time, no one made their usual jokes. Eyes fixed as busy hands made ready whilst their minds flitted from anxious uncertainty to adrenaline-fuelled strength.

'You know what... if this is really going to happen,' Jimi started, 'let's drink on it, tonight. Toast it all. Make sense of our new reality.'

'What if they come at us, Jimi?' Tammy said, already moving to the bar.

'Ain't anyone stupid enough to brave that storm brewing. And if they do, there's a heavier one in you two waiting to rain down on them — that's for sure.'

Jack sat cross-legged. A Buddha at peace with the world that was in turmoil about him. The girls, Jimi, and their crews, working the island, were tight. The closest family he'd wish to have. Everyone had each other's back. It was alien to Jack until recent days. Now he welcomed its embrace like a mug of coffee in a morning's hot shower after a hard night's graft.

Jack shot up. 'Now then, what y' having? Take a seat, Tammy. This one's on me.'

'Don't mind if I do.'

The storm raised up and raged like the temper of a mad man. Like Max Ballard. It battered the Inn's window shutters, the hospital, lookouts and the shoreline as giant waves came cutting through the darkness. The moon highlighted the sea's crests as her waves came crashing down again and again. Smashing black horses at her peaks attacking the ancient coastline.

They drank and cheered this, their new existence. Hi-lighted and celebrated by nature's unsympathetic torments outside.

'Your brother, Jimi?' Betty said, looking to the floor through a glass of Grey Goose, straight up.

'We don't talk. He went his way. I went mine. We were close...but not. No real bad blood between us. Just the half-blood we did share. Mothers. Was diluted by her taking our fathers not being there, out on us.'

'Where'd he go?'

'Jack son. That's just it. Where didn't he go? He's a dark bastard son of a...'

'Jimi!' Tammy interrupted.

'Sorry, I guess… But she really was. John took our surname to heart. Black by name. A *Heart of darkness* by nature. He's been at war, over there, and here… Biggest ones are always inside though. I've hammered mine out on site after site. He's got scars,' Jimi played with his own scar on his wrist. A lasting token from a building site he worked on five years ago. He was drilling a bit of metal in a vice, making a new door hinge. The vice lost its grip and the freshly cut metal section span like helicopter blades into his wrist, missing his radial artery by millimetres.

'Why don't you call him?' Tammy said.

'Don't have his number. And he wouldn't answer...'

'Would he make it worse? Darker than Ballard?' Jack said.

'He got burned up pretty bad in Ireland. Refused to fire back. Saw ghosts in the flames. Our ghosts. He's true to his core. And one day we'll see each other again. Not like this though. Those ghosts he sees. The same ones will help us win this.'

And no one mentioned him again, John Black and his ghosts were too heavy and serious for this caper. They all felt it.

Twenty-Three

MAX MARCHED HIS MEN through a wall of wind and rain towards a harbour at the end of the seafront. He'd been so on track, focussed, the weather didn't dent his actions. His men, now terrified of the sea, took it in turns to mutter to each other when Max was out of earshot.

'He's gonna get us all killed,' the oldest, Trevor, said.

Didn't think I'd go out like this,' a younger one said, 'drowned at sea like a fucking wet rat. I'm practically breathing it in here: rancid. Polluted. Bristol Channel piss,' he continued.

Trevor nodded at him, they were all resigned to the fact; mother nature's driving wind and waters were measurable, sure to fade. But father Ballard's would never back down.

The crazy three brothers stayed near to Max Ballard. Like old Western henchmen. Closest to Max, last to fall. They were a human body vest at times. They knew it. And with the feeling of threat from the wind, rain, and sea, it was obvious the gang was less than eager. Not a hundred per cent behind the idea of going on the water for some petty tit for tat one-upmanship bollocks Max had conjured up as an excuse to go on this, his latest rappage. The brothers imagined mutiny in the ranks.

They all stopped in a bus shelter by the bay. Boat ropes clattered against masts as bells rang out in a din of wind.

'Gather round, pussies.'

'Okay, lads, you heard the man, gather round,' The Narrator said, pulling up his collar fifteen minutes too late, already soaked through.

'Gather round,' went The Echo.

'GET IN LINE,' Last Orders finished.

'Here it comes, a fucking pep talk,' the younger lad from earlier muttered.

Max sprang at him with a cobra's reflex and a bull's mass. The lad was dragged, feet kicking, over the road and over the edge of the bay walls. He had him by one foot as the lad screamed, dangling and whimpering. 'You don't make me son. The weather doesn't. And...it won't break me either. But I can you,' and he teetered him like a young calf in the grip of a crocodile over a cliff edge — damned either way. Querying on each fragile moment; the lesser of pains as options to *go out*.

And then you could see it in the boy's face. Like the young calf at the potential fate of a cliff versus a crocodile's teeth and jaws. He now welcomed the drop. Fearing Ballard's grip and bite more than the drop.

Ballard flexed, muscles taut. He reached a spare arm up as if to embrace the forces of nature like he was one with it; part of the family. 'You don't get off that easy, piss-weasel,' and he threw him to the road.

The boy scampered back. Then stood up straight. Like an army cadet caught with his laces undone. He brushed the mud from his trench coat and stuck his chest out: a soldier again.

Loyalty and duty tended to win over in The Cricketers. Max had rescued them from the swamp of life, like birds with broken wings. It didn't take much reminding.

Max Ballard yelled through the rain, his words piercing the drops like they were bullets. 'This isn't about me, you or even them... What's it all going to come to when a group of builders, plumbers and sparkies are standing up to South Bank London gangsters?! What's next? I'll tell you what… Fucking old ladies with shopping trollies giving us shit.'

There were elbow nudges and stifled sniggers in the ranks at the mention of the old dear that had cracked one of the brothers in the shin.

Ballard's roar against the weather continued, 'It's gone on too long. The shifting tides towards virtual online criminality has taken its toll. On all of us: the foot soldiers working the same old beat. No one takes us seriously anymore. Except me,' waves crashed on his every word. Lightning cracked as the rain came in horizontally, and the bus shelter was fruitless as a barrier against it, creaking and groaning.

'On that island, lies our recompense,' Max ushered towards a crescendo.

One of the lads from the back muttered, 'What's that mean?'

'Means we're getting even wetter,' one answered.

'On that island, lies our respect,' Max pointed.

'Why?' another muttered, out of earshot and drowned out by the storm.

'On. That. Island. Lies our future. Now you can either take it now. Or roll over and we'll forever be underdogs to the common labourer. Whipping dogs to the next passing old lady,' he found a roar above the weather, 'NOW… TAKE IT!' and he turned, pointed his fist at it like a fisted Nazi salute.

They took a plywood landing craft that used to take occasional loads of tourists across. It was the nearest boat big enough to fit them and proud enough for Max's ego, even though Max wasn't joining them. *He* intended on commanding the one boat fleet from the shore, sitting in the bus shelter like a misplaced ancient Greek commander. When they'd landed and taken the rock, he would retreat to the bar and toast his new addition to an empire with Japanese whiskey.

If the crazy three brothers weren't on board and they hadn't all been raised by Max's words, the rest would have just pointed the boat at Wales and tuned their drenched backs on it all. There would be a limit to the blind loyalty. The self-sacrifices. As always Max had reminded them, shouted to the boat as it pulled away: if they weren't there, with him, doing what he saw had to be done, they weren't anybody, anywhere.

Sadly again, they believed it.

He'd picked half of them up off their knees on the streets. The rest had willingly approached him for work. Their lives didn't matter beforehand. He'd given something back to them even if now they were at the mercy of the sea. And the boat seemed like a cork bobbing on deep waters coated in fires.

Lights glimmered in the distance on the island as the Cricketer's boat bobbed and smashed through the waves. Lights appeared onshore. Lanterns, torches, then something else lit up in the water on the island's shore up ahead. A beacon of light, a warning, or a mermaid's curse.

'What the fuck is that?' said a lad near the bow as he peered over the edge of the boat under an arm attempting to shelter a head already soaked.

'Looks big,' another said.

'Bigger than us,' came a smaller voice.

The Narrator pointed from the helm at the back. Stood either side of him, The Echo and Last Orders shook their heads slowly then held on the sides tight. Thoughts started at the tiller, with The Narrator's shaking hands as he looked down but steered on: what had they all gotten into? How had it got so messed up? The South Bank Cricketers had gone, in only a few days, from respected London gangsters working the streets of the big city to drowned out old, tired rodents, bobbing around in a leaking wooden barrel chugging along, barely managing to push through the waves and weather. Let alone face whatever *that* was up ahead. And *it* was getting closer. Brighter. Bigger.

***

Jimi mused into a fire that feigned warming the spot the girls were preparing to leave behind. 'Dying birds and sinking ships won't stop them now. No longer are us and them, magnets trying to force north against north, repelled. Now we're melding together. Our metal is as one.'

Tammy and Betty busied in the background, as the sea battle got closer, looming outside. Only Jack and Jimi had the headspace to consider the exploded pieces of all their lives all melting together. The girls were fixed on adrenaline and a strength of ages, layering up as each second passed.

'We should go with the girls,' Jack said looking at Tammy and Betty. His words seemed weakened as Tammy's arms strengthened, flexing as her tattoos reached out like demons with each crack of the lighting.

Like a wildcat Betty used to be scared of water — shear terrified. As a child, she was seen as an effeminate boy, and so was berated and bullied for her look and ways. She'd been pushed to dive under in an icy Northern river. A boy jumped in from a tree and landed on her as she struggled to the surface. She lay on the bottom, glazed over, staring at the rocks, algae, and small stones for what felt her own, forever. Her lungs burned but her body wouldn't move. She was panicked but paralysed, stuck to the bottom — watching over her own slow death. Another boy dove down and pulled her up. Not to rescue her but because he thought she was hiding, playing a game. As they punched and kicked her to wake her, by some fluke they hit the right spot. That never left her. The water's touch. Or her unsympathetic revival by the boys as they walked away and left her throwing up. She was some disposable plaything to the boys, even back then, before her transformation into true self as a woman...

'This is our time,' Betty said, picking up a harpoon from the floor, rapping a rag around the end and dipping it in a pot of oil and lighter fluid mix — her past was buried, her time was now.

'You boys take care here, we need somewhere to fall back to. And they might go around us. We'll take some of the *crews* here with us,' Tammy said.

Their crews were already on shore with Old Rosie waiting.

'But...' Jack said.

'Keep the home fires burning,' Betty said. And they both stared down at the men who were now reduced to boys, their bruised wet faces looked back in pure admiration. The women were resolute, unwavering. Stronger than the seas and rains that raged outside.

The Cricketers didn't stand a chance. They were *out for zero*.

***

Max watched his own crew's boat leave shore.

In the distance, a dim light from the island appeared then slowly grew in intensity. A haunting glow, looming and threatening. As The Cricketers' boat neared a central patch of water between land and island it stopped. Time froze. Rain and wind seized.

Then it began.

The sea and skies were lit up. Arcs of light emblazoned the sky as lines of rain were lit like lasers cutting down into the waves and the boat below.

'What the f...' Max stuttered as his phone exploded in messages, lighting up and vibrating in unison with the light show up ahead. He sat on the bus shelter bench read them out loud:

The Narrator: *'Boss, there's something big headed our way. Lights and fire.'*
The Echo: *'Flames!'*
Last Orders: *'Angry Viking war-goddesses. Demons.'*

Max shook his head, closed his eyes, and went into another place in his head. It was a place without the fighting, storms, rain, and torrential downpour of shit that had swept up and was now all around them all. It was a place without Weston. It was a place where his wife was.

'Give it up, Max. You're told old. You were never that good at playing the hard man. We all know who really wore the trousers,' she said. 'Now, just give it up... Get back to living. I'll see you soon enough.'

A defeated man, Max slowly stood up. Eyes still closed. When he opened them the storm was dulling and the moon had taken over the night sky. The mass of the large vessel had disappeared and the wreckage of The Cricketer's had about turned and looked to be returning, like a damp limp dick, back to shore.

Max thought, whatever was out there must have been something to make them want to come back to shore to face me. After failure. Something had changed. He'd have expected them to scarper and make for Wales in their disintegrating craft and take their chances with the Bristol Channel, rather than rush back to his awaiting wrath. Instead, they made their way back like little boys done bad. To take the belt strap. Knowing a father's angry embrace would surely follow.

Max knew it. There'd be no belt strap. The words from his wife's ghost had tempered a beast inside. She'd given him strength whilst she was alive. And now, in death, she took it.

He headed back to the bar.

This was over — they were all out sure enough. It was a short test match; a failed innings. He had to make a plan, restore a momentum some other way. She'd already crept back into his head. Started at him like a rabid dog. He wasn't ready for that, not yet. They'd re-join soon enough. Not yet, he thought.

Not now, pet.

Twenty-Four

MAX DRANK A THIRD LARGE HIBIKI, straight, and leant on the serving side of the bar, waiting for his mind to deliver him from soberness and a darkened night's torment. Drips from the window frame outside reminded him of the storm that had raged. Could still. And it resounded their defeat. Now anything and nothing was possible. He looked down through the amber glass to the scratched bar top below.

A shadow entered. Assuming it was one his crew that was back, wet, and with a tail between their legs, he didn't look up to see.

'Take a seat. It's over.'

'You're right there,' said the dripping shadow of John Black — Jimi's brother.

Max jumped, his eyes opened wide, a stare stretched his lids, letting the world in. His hand scrambled for his Glock under the bar.

John sat calmly on a stool facing Max.

As a history of violence passed in moments as Max lifted, hesitantly resting his hand holding the Glock on the bar and pointed it firmly at John. This history was where John was set up by a copper, when he was meant to be hiding away on Witness Protection. He was set up to catch Max's brother Sean Ballard. Now residing at her Majesty's pleasure. This same history...Max had ignored. Because John had grown into the shoes of Mr Big in Manchester, through some twist of fate, and had all the major Manchester rival gangs and the police in his pocket. He was a dark overlord, on neither side. Worst still, he fucking documented his mind's actions in books and Max didn't want to be in one.

'Manchester's a long way from Weston, John.'

'Maybe, but you forget where it all started. For us, anyhow... Even though we've never met. It was in Bristol, Max,' and John put his hands on the bar. A show of strength at being unarmed. An arrogant or confident move, it had Max shaking at the knee. He didn't let it show above the bar. 'Seen your brother recently?'

'We weren't close...'

'Neither me to mine,' and one of John's eyebrows twitched and his head tilted ever slow slightly.

Max puzzled, then a penny dropped, 'Jimi?'

John's hands moved fast. Putting them to the bar wasn't a show of weakness it was nearing them for a strike. A well-practiced move, he had one hand over the gun with a finger behind the guard, pressing hard at Max's finger that bruised and cracked. He couldn't squeeze. And the other had Max's drinking hand pulled forward. His head and face followed and John stared deep into Max's eyes.

There, Max saw wars, pains and demons way beyond his making.

Fade to black.

Outside, Max's recently de-faced driver started the engine of a transit van. It wasn't far to the seafront but Max was big, and they didn't want to take the risk being seen dragging him along. Besides, they wanted to sweat him first, to think about what had brought him to this point. That's why they brought the ropes, knives, and pictures of his wife. John knew something of Max, Pat had filled in the rest, enough to push the right buttons.

Without confidence in how much of a liability John Black was or wasn't, Pat waited in the shadows. He saw punches. Blood. The ropes came out. Max was hog-tied. And the van door opened and slammed shut. With it, Pat's anxiety skyrocketed. What had he done? Giving over an empire to Black.

His would surely follow.

Twenty-Five

THE TWO WOMEN LEFT.

Jimi sat touching the floor they'd walked across, stroking the wet stains left behind in boot prints on ancient dusty floorboards. He touched his fingers to his lips and imagined all their futures, together. If they could get through the next few minutes, hours...and days. He imagined hard-drinking, parties, and guests. Lots of sleepovers. Love ruled and it was a safe place. No one looked to battle and beat each other, on or off the island. Everyone was in harmony with the place, each other, and life. He thought on his past trips to Sand Point, to rectify and settle his woes. He'd replace this ritual with lone fishing trips to the opposite side of the island. And he'd return with a bounty of food, fish — substance. Unlike his previous trips to The Point where the best they got back was his temporarily unladen troubles — a washed mind.

'They're about to cast off. Let's go, watch it from shore,' Jack said looking through the shutters.

Jimi stood, patted Jack's back, and turned him towards the door. He couldn't remember if he'd done it before — held, touched him, or offered anything a father should. It was early days for that. It was late days too: a lot to make up for.

'Let's go, *son*.'

Jack's face and eyes were the last to shift after his body led the way. He didn't want to miss a thing.

A crack of lightning beckoned them down the old stone passage as Jimi bounced off the walls on the way down. People were smaller *back then* and Jimi was an ox by comparison.

***

The waves bobbed, crashing, as the wind tore through them as they unleashed fires of hell from harpoons wrapped in oily rags. Arcs of fire lit up the night sky — a melee of veins cutting through the darkness...slicing windows through the night's blackness to the other side and whatever lay beyond in space and time.

As the girls' boat, Old Rodie, attacked. All of them on The Cricketers' craft were in sheer panic. The girls and their crew could see the frenzied rats battling the flames, waters and weather as it all rained down on them, in biblical measures, relentlessly. Looking to drown their sorry souls.

Old Rosie had her row of outboard motors doing the hard work, the black sails were more for menace but added a hard added push with the fierce winds behind her. The pirate ship mast with black sails loomed like a ghost through the waters. A dirty white flag on top blew furiously displaying a black crow. This was for Jimi. He would joke that a crow followed him everywhere he went. Sometimes it was a friend, other times it was a dark omen. As a child, they seemed to follow him around. Deep croaky voices in agreement and sometimes a warning. His school *friends* would shoot them with air rifles, given the chance. Most of the kids at his school had some deep-seated resentment of nature, authority, and each other. Anyone to lay the blame on for being poor and their parents taking the same out on them. It was a vicious circle of angst and Jimi as a minority in his loyalty, confidence and wanting to do *right*. He stopped one lad pulling the trigger on a nest of ravens. It was like shooting fish in a barrel really. The chicks wouldn't be ready to fly for a few days, maybe weeks and the mother wouldn't abandon the chicks. The evilness in the lad simmered away as he took his spot, waited, took his time firing idle pellets into the nest to torment and take them out. Jimi, only 7 years old at the time, crept up behind the older lad, stamped on the rifle, then he bent the gun in two the wrong way — stamped again through it. The older boy was in disbelief, then started to flay and hit at Jimi.

Then the birds came.

The older lad was pecked and Jimi did the rest. Since then he saw crows and jet-black ravens in everyone and everything. He saw them in the colour of Betty's hair. It became a welcome omen.

For The Cricketers, the crow on the flag was their end.

'The wind is tearing at us!' Brian shouted to Betty and Tammy, 'It'll have us in the drink.'

Mikey and Stevie wrestled over the four boats that were fixed together that made up The Rosie and handled her mast and boom, trying to calm the sails from tearing them apart. They made ready their hands on her to release them from the wind's grasp, looking up for the women's command to set them free.

'It's going to have us over. We need to cut the sail loose,' Brian shouted as the other two hugged, gripped and pulled at the angry mast, pulleys and boom.

Tammy and Betty both nodded. Betty waved her hands as her jet-black hair danced in the moonlight and Tammy turned the Tiller back towards the island. They'd made their point: crippled The Cricketers boat, forcing them to retreat back to dry land, with tails between their legs, if they stayed afloat in the storm. Now Old Rosie was creaking, groaning, and battling the wind and waves. They needed to turn whilst they were still topside too.

Stevie released the pulley and Mikey ducked as the boom swang like an angry giant boxer's heavy-laden arm and iron fist. Then it came back at them, and again they ducked.

'That was a close one,' Mikey shouted.

'Too close,' yelled Brian. Eyes wide. Dripping with the sea and a deep fear that soon took them all.

The three men looked back, jerking their gaze to where *she* had stood.

Betty was gone.

Twenty-Six

I N A MOMENT, SOMETHING MUCH DARKER than the night had taken their hearts.

From the shore Jack and Jimi looked on, feeling it too as a blanket of despair spread from Old Rosie, across the waters and touched the island.

Tammy and the men bobbed around, circling best they could, looking to each wave and blast of spray for the gift that wouldn't come. They wanted Betty back from the sea that had taken her.

Jack pulled Jimi back from diving in — tears and angst ripped through both their faces.

All felt lost.

***

They scoured the shore for an eternity, searching and taking it in turns to pull Jimi back from entering the violent waters himself.

Later, the light and heat from the inn's fire couldn't touch them. Their world had become a cold dark hole with no way out. All of them sat on the floor, heavy drinks lay untouched in front of them like sacrificial hearts to be squeezed when the time was right. As the moon's grip over sea and land dropped, it seemed no time would ever be right.

By the time the sun started to rise only Brian's drink had been touched, a mere sip by his standards. More an automated reflex than a conscious effort on his part to be disrespectful.

A faint noise came. They all jumped up.

As the door to the inn slowly creaked and moved the

crack of its opening caught dust in the air.

She entered the room like a moving painting, an image of womanhood — relentless strength.

'That's getting to be quite a habit,' Betty said to Jimi's face full of tears. 'You ol' soft bastard.' Then they were all on her in an embrace so tight she thought she might burst... 'Wait, wait, just a minute' and she pushed them away.

'What? Too good for us now...you settled with a seal overnight or something?' said Jimi.

'I wasn't the only thing that washed ashore,' Betty said as a grin grew to fill the room with excitement. 'There's something I need to show you before it gets eaten by the birds.'

***

John and Max's ex-driver, Danny, took the Max shaped bundle of arms and legs to the water's edge. At first, Max thought that was it, he was getting dropped in the drink. Bye-bye coastal sideline in Weston, hello dead berating wife.

It wasn't going to be that easy.

John leant down low, whispered into Max's ear, 'You know me. Where I'm from. What happened to my predecessor. They're still picking bits of him out of the tarmac below the tower block. AND do you know who I've got in my pocket? Fu-cki-ing ev-ry-one,' John spelt it out, plain as day so there was no confusion. 'I'm taking you over there,' John pointed over the waters, 'delivering you to my brother, Jimi.'

Max's eyes opened wide in the dark realisation of the tangled web he'd been shaking like an idle blue bottle before the black widow returned. John Black was Jimi's brother and Max had stoked a dangerous fire. Max thought how fucking poetic it all was. Pat had fucking known and played him too

— the west country snake. Max didn't want to be out of the game, not like this. He'd had enough, his eyes rolled over then back again. They went away fearful and in shock and came back conceding defeat. He was done.

John Black had made his point, but he finished Max off, just to be sure, '...don't know what he's going to do with you over there. Damn sure it's a fraction of what I'll do if I have to come back. And next time, I'll bring all of Manchester's finest, above and below the line, with me,' John unbuttoned and pulled the top of his shirt down. There was an old inky SAS tattoo on one side, scars, an underground record label tattoo synonymous with Manchester's underground and most infamous club, and then there were more scars.

John didn't mention he was in bed with the police too, literally. Cherry was a force to be reckoned with in her own right. There was no need to drop that bomb. He kept a tone with Max knowing John had toppled an empire up north, and *his* was next.

The wind and waters had stilled from earlier as the moon retreated and the sun strained to replace it, cresting its head. Reflecting a blood-red sheen over the oily black stillness of the Channel's horizon. Max closed his eyes as John and Danny loaded him into a small boat, started the motor and set off to deliver him.

John could see in Max's eyes. He was resigned to his fate. John had broken bigger backs. He also knew it could be an act, so to be sure he bent over and whispered words to Max's shivering head. By the time he was dumped on the shore of the island, he'd be well tenderised and ready for Jimi.

A seagull cried out, shat like a pterodactyl, just missing the side of their boat. The splash made ripples. Danny noticed more up ahead, something was in the water.

'What's that?' Danny said to John and the sea.

John looked up from Max, under his boot. He rested a hand on the edge of the boat and strained to see what Danny was looking at. It was a body, laid flat. How you're trained to if you go in the drink, lose the energy to swim on and hope for rescue.

'Get closer,' John pointed but Danny was steering there already, moving them slowly towards the shape in the water — the body of Betty Jardin.

'Is she...?' Danny muttered as they pulled her in, thinking the worst.

'She's the right colour,' John started, touched her forehead and hands for temperature and then neck and wrist for a pulse. 'She's still going strong. A strong miracle.'

One of her eyes opened, and saw John looking down, 'Jimi?'

'No, not Jimi. We'll take you to him — it's his lucky day: two for the price of one,' John said and nudged Max with his heel.

Betty closed her eyes. John and Danny took off their coats and put them over her. It would be a short journey for Max. Too short. For Betty, it would be an eternity.

John looked out at the island, thinking of his brother. They'd been apart most their lives but somehow always there. Now it counted, John couldn't be more present. He only hoped he could make the drop without Jimi finding out. He feared it would only harbour resentment in his brother. That John had had to interfere. Even worse that Pat had made the call on his behalf, not Jimi himself.

'Do you know who I am?' John said to Betty, lifting her to shore.

'No.'

'Let's keep it that way.'

Whilst Max was still inside the boat and hidden from

Betty's view, John leant in, over the edge, took something out of his pocket, folded it and put in Max's shirt. He patted it and looked into Max's eyes like whatever it was he now had in his pocket was a last will. Danny never left the boat as he bundled Max up and John pulled him over the edge and onto the sand and stones below.

'Thanks,' said Betty as the boat started to pull away,

'It ain't over yet,' John said, looking to the heap on the sand that was now the tamed monster: Max Ballard.

As the boat got further away Betty thought how she felt she'd recognised the man who'd pulled her from the sea. Soon her mind went to the demon on the sands. The source of their pains. She lifted her leg back to crack him in the face and he winced. And she stopped, her boot hovering an inch from his nose. Then she knelt in the sand next to him.

'What have you done to yourself, silly little man? You're just an old city gangster. A dinosaur. You just destroy. Jimi's something else. A force. A maker. A creator — he's a fucking builder. '

Max had nothing. He was actually starting to agree with her.

Betty thought of rolling him into the sea or digging a hole and putting him in it. There was someone she needed to see first; her heart pined. It was Jimi's call to make. Betty stood and walked towards the Inn steps and just hoped he wouldn't do anything to make things worse.

Twenty-Seven

'I KNOW JUST THE PLACE,' said Jack, as they all looked down at Max.

'Oh, yes. Perfect,' Jimi said. 'Girls, saddle up Old Rosie for another ride. We've a long drop from a fiery rope for our friend here, and we don't want to keep old Brunel's bridge waiting,' as Jimi bent down and grabbed Max, a note fell from his pocket, and then a playing card.

The note:

> *'Consider my debt paid for the time you did for us.*
> *Love, Pat.'*

'That figures,' Jimi said.

Max looked up, seeing the dots joining up with the note and card Jimi held. It's what Pat hadn't told him in the diner that now deafened him. Pat Lynch, and the Bristol crew, knew Jimi's brother was John Black. It was their fall back, leverage. Pat, the fucker didn't even have to dirty his hands. Damn it, Max thought, did Pat even pay for that coffee in the diner?

Jimi turned the card: Jack of Spades. There was more to this. Jimi knew his brother was nearby, involved, part of it. Ever since they were kids, his brother, John, used playing cards to mark books he read and those he was writing — it was his marker.

Max closed his eyes over and over again. Trying to open up to a new more acceptable illusion each time. When he opened them the first, he was on another boat. Next, the back of a van. It didn't work, the illusion just kept getting worse. The next time he opened up, he was upside down, hung like a prize catch, a sorry tired, beaten shark. The blood rushed to his head, now feeling like a lead weight.

Then... he was over the edge, tape ripped from his mouth for a last confession as he dangled 75 meters above the mud slurry of the Avon Gorge. Four unsympathetic faces looked down on him from the railings. And the least, Jimi, held the rope as Jack had a Zippo lighter, clicking it open and shut.

Max smelt the lighter fluid all over him.

Tammy smiled.

Betty too, 'Sorry, little man,' she said. Winking in a way only a stripper could. Able to rouse a reaction in the most inappropriate moment. She liked that - was well-practiced at it.

As his balls tightened, he was bitter at his body's response, and Max lashed out, 'Betty-bitch! You're just a punch drunk ladyboy. Have you even told any of them you used to be a fucking man?' Max seethed upside-down as his rage redirected the blood back to his face from his shamed regions.

They all shrugged. It didn't matter, Betty's past didn't matter or that he knew it, not any more than the light rain that tickled and cleaned their faces.

'Sounds like a shit-hot name for a band, 'Jack said.

Jimmy feigned dropping Max's sorry ass as they giggled. He let the rope slip just a little. Then added, 'Damn, that really is... A good name for a band.'

It started with Betty, then Tammy, Jimi, Jack… They all cracked up giggling, laughing. The rain stopped before it had really started and there was a glimmer of light as a star broke a point in the night sky. A bead of blood-mixed sweat gathered on Max's upturned nose, built to a pressure-filled drop, then fell. The river below them all shifted as the droplet hit water and a pair of swans flew gracefully under the bridge gasping as they went. A couple for life, on to their next place. Max felt the imbalance in himself shift, a 'new normal' took hold and he eventually cracked up as well. His broken demeanour returned and with it he defrosted and joined them. Soon tears of laughter left his blood heavy crimson face. And they were all left cracking up at the absurdity they'd made with life in such short a time.

'Keep the island. And play the bar — it's gone to shit without you,' Max said as they started to pull.

'Punch Drunk Lady Boy gets its first gig then,' Jimi said.

They pulled him back up and with each length of the rope, they brought themselves back to reality. None of them was cut out for this shit anymore. Max least of all and they knew he knew it too.

***

Max had underestimated Jimi and his reach. He didn't have him down as much of a criminal but knew now he could pull the whole house of cards down in a flash. Max had plans anyhow, and with someone — he just didn't know how to break it to Jimi, that it was with his ex-wife.

She was turning up soon, Max had to think quick.

Max knew nothing could ever stop Jimi taking the stage. Nothing. Not even the bomb he was about to drop. So, when Jimi was kissing his favourite plectrum and about to head up, Max whispered in his ear, 'I knew her, your ex. In fact, we were a bit of a thing for a night or so…. Sorry.'

'Suits you. Both of you. Match made in hell,' Jimi said through a half-smile. In sympathy of Max as much as in showing no issue with it.

A shadow of John Black loomed from outside,

reminding Max of his new civilian path. The one he was to stay on if he was to stay alive; not meet up with her indoors (and underground) just yet. He had someone else now, to help with that. The door opened behind Jimi as he walked up to the stage so he couldn't see his ex-wife walking up to Max. Not until he was plugged in and facing the audience. His ex-wife kissed Max. And Jack, who'd been leant nearby on the bar, looked confused. He looked to Jimi then back to his mother with Max.

Jimi played an opening E-Minor and let it hang in the air. His feedback re-christened the room. He looked out over his domain. Jack's puzzled face caught his eye and he followed his gaze over to Max who now stood arm and arm with Jimi's ex.

Jack looked back at Jimi and saw he was at peace. Everything was in its right place. Tammy and Betty went over to Jack and the room lit up as the walls bent and the lights flickered with a braying attack of Jimi's blue's rock guitar. He finished the intro to Back in Black.

Outside John looked in, silhouetted by the streetlights. He stayed for the full set. At the end of the night, there was a mini pile of finished rollies and seven empty tumblers on the cobbles outside where Tammy had left the double Jameson.

As he packed up his guitar and walked into the night Jimi felt a familiar shadow.

'Good set, bro… Loved Back in Black.'

'You would,' Jimi said, '…you would. Keep me out of the damn book.'

'See you at the funeral?'

Jimi didn't answer.

They both leant back on the window and looked at the deep blackness on the other side of the alley.

Jimi thought about how to put it to his brother he

hadn't seen since they cut their knees and scraped elbows climbing trees as children. He remembered the time John had cut his finger to the bone. He didn't wince much but there was a lot of blood. When he pulled the skin back and they saw the ivory bone they both turned pale, ran home to the anger and lack of sympathy. Jimi put an arm around him that time, the only time. Filling in where their mother wouldn't.

Eventually, Jimi asked, 'Why did they fire you, from the army... the SAS?'

'I wouldn't fire back. Decided I'd rather be shot than shoot back at the Irish, or anyone just on their say so. Didn't matter what politic or church thought different.'

Jimi paused, digested the air between them and blew smoke. 'You see, John, for me, when I was up north, I'd take their words, full of fire, all the time. Like I was the problem. I've resigned myself to be out of range to them. To be down here now.'

John nodded, 'I'll take the hit for you. And go to the funeral. Just save me a bolt hole on that island... I might need it sometime.'

Jimi nodded back. They smoked. Drank to the bottom of the glass they were on like it was a shared peace pipe, then John left, like he always did, devoured by night.

Twenty-Eight

J IMI PLAYED GUITAR. He was okay, not great... better than the rest.

His name had been removed from above the door but the place was still his, and the girls'. You could stick whatever plastic plaque over the top but their names were chiselled into the walls, bar and floor of that place. The new blood sweat and tears really didn't matter; it was the things they'd done beforehand that had won the peoples' hearts and minds.

Max had changed its name back; it was the Hell's Belles again. He knew his place in the new machine. 'Why throw the baby out with the dishwater,' as his mother used to say. Prioritising dirty dishes over a child's body. She was a hard woman and he never considered that she might have just fucked up the old saying.

Jimi re-broke the ice on his first night back. In the following week's set Jack warmed them up with a bit of T.N.T. and High Voltage, then the girls took them to boiling point with burlesque bar-top titty twirls and face slaps to stoke the flames. Then Jimi blew the roof off. Everything was sure in its right place again. Jimi, Jack, Tammy and Betty had the island with the occasional day-vacation to shore. And Jimi's brother, John, returned to his underworld.

***

'I mean it,' said a voice on a hands-free mobile laying in several day's ashes, papers and spilt wine over a cheap Northern hotel room's table, 'make me harder, younger and better looking than Pat and Jimi when you write it.'

'We'll see,' John said typing hard through a wall of smoke, 'you know how it goes though, a leopard can't change its spots. But you can always do it a favour with a Bowie knife…' He paused, stopped typing, and made a note to himself.

Max breathed a sigh of resignation on the line.

'…and skin it,' John stated.

Max hung on the gravity of the words.

'Don't kill me off. I'm not ready to go back to her yet. I've found someone else.'

'We'll see, Max… Maybe next time.'

Printed in Great Britain
by Amazon

62434689R00102